D1569657

GUNDOWN

**Center Point
Large Print**

**This Large Print Book carries the
Seal of Approval of N.A.V.H.**

GUNDOWN

LAURAN PAINE

CENTER POINT PUBLISHING
THORNDIKE, MAINE

This Center Point Large Print edition
is published in the year 2009 by arrangement with
Golden West Literary Agency.

The text of this Large Print edition is unabridged.
In other aspects, this book may vary
from the original edition.
Printed in the United States of America.
Set in 16-point Times New Roman type.

ISBN: 978-1-60285-401-7

Library of Congress Cataloging-in-Publication Data

Paine, Lauran.
  Gundown / Lauran Paine. -- Center Point large print ed.
     p. cm.
  Originally published under the name: Russ Thompson.
  ISBN 978-1-60285-401-7 (lib. bdg. : alk. paper)
  1. Large type books. I. Thompson, Russ, 1916- Gundown. II. Title.

PS3566.A34G844 2009
813'.54--dc22

2008045806

GUNDOWN

ONE
A Returning at Springtime

The day Edson Black returned and confronted his two sons, Big Bill was shocked. He felt a flooding sorrow. He had not seen his father in seven years, since they had taken him to Yuma in the prison wagon, but it might as well have been thirty years so old and worn-out did he now seem.

Jess leaned upon a porch upright stonily impassive except for his midnight eyes which moved, caught all movement, all light and shadow. He was the younger, and also by half a head the shorter, but even so Jess was taller and thicker than the man with his Pa, Sheriff Blake Hobart from town, who, after putting down the old man's sack-wrapped effects, straightened up, gray and solid and strong, to eye both the sons then to turn and push out a hand towards the father.

"Rest," he softly told Edson Black, because it was still a shock to see what they had sent back from Yuma Prison, and because a lawman did not have to like a man he had worked hard to send away, he only had to *know* him; the man they had come for was not at all like this wasted ruin they had sent back.

"Just go fishin' a little, Ed, and maybe ride the foothills."

Sheriff Hobart did not look back at the stalwart sons out front of the log house as he turned,

7

climbed in, lifted the lines and clucked at his buggy-horse. He did not look back once he was beyond the yard, either. He simply wanted to get away from that atmosphere back there, return to Frontera. He should not have had a sensation of guilt but he *had* one, for while he had done exactly what his duty had required of him, and no more, what the lady he served—Justice—had done down at Yuma made him feel badly about being a part of that same system.

Ed Black smiled up at his big sons, moving ahead towards the porch, his thrusting, strong stride gone and in its place a dogged shuffle. The angular face was gray and tired, the throat-muscles hung turkey-neck slack and the bushy head of hair was down to a thinning thatch.

He shook young Jess's big bronzed hand. "Boy, you've come on. You look uncommonly like your Maw." He turned as Big Bill the elder strode over, face stone-set to hide the pain in Bill's gray eyes. The gripping hand was palsied but its strength was adequate as the old man turned his fogging gaze. "How have the cattle done, son, and the horses? It's something I was never sure I'd be able to do—stand here like this. . . . And your Maw—is buried over in the pines. Directly I'd like to go over there. Well, Bill. . . . ?"

"We have some cattle left, Paw, and a few heads of the horses you was breeding up. Jess'll rig up the wagon and take you around this afternoon."

8

"Well, son, maybe in the morning? I'm plumb wore down. It's been a long day."

Towering Big Bill absently nodded and looked past at younger Jess. Their eyes briefly touched then Jess went out to pick up the burlap bundles and fetch them inside the house.

Bill filled the room. He left this impression in almost any building including the saloon, the general store in town. He was four inches above being six feet tall, weighed over two hundred and fifteen pounds, it took a stout horse to carry him and a big meal to settle his requirements after day-long work. He was thirty this spring. Jess was twenty-four and weighed just two hundred. It was solid, punched-down weight well proportioned over a heavy-boned six-foot frame, and Jess did in fact have his mother's dark hair and eyes, her golden half-breed coloring, her basic mannerisms and her periods of pensive silence.

Big Bill was his father's son right down to the angular face and gun-metal eyes. He was more open and outright than Jess, less quick to turn fierce, and lighter with his hands on the hair-rope reins of colts.

He was also a deadly man with weapons, so what his size did not do towards discouraging antagonists, his reputation with guns usually did.

He stood now in the dingy cabin's wide parlor and listened as his father's fading voice faintly rang with pleasure.

"There's nothing a man thinks of but his home, boys, and nothing is greater to him than his family. Well . . ." he turned slowly, but all—nearly all—trace of a woman's hand had been obliterated long ago. His wife had died that first year he'd been 'down there'. The bachelor boys had lived here alone since. Seven years was a long period of time.

He turned back with his fading brave smile. "Well, still and all I'm close to her here. Closer than I'd be anywhere else."

They took him to the bedroom no one had used since the passing of his wife, left him to lie down for a couple of hours, went trooping out front to the porch where Jess turned with wet-scalded black eyes and said, "Gawd a'mighty. . . ."

Big Bill sat upon a bench pushing out great oaken legs. "Well; we've heard how they're treated down there."

"But he was strong as a bull when he went away. Big, and strong as a bull."

The elder brother turned and slowly searched the face of the darkest one. "It's been done," he said, and lowered his head. "Gawd I never figured he'd look like this—but it's done and over, Jess."

"And so we sit here like a pair of sheep?"

"What do you expect? There's no way to turn things back. We've been talkin' about this ever since he left. Jess; it's finished. There is not a blessed thing folks can do now. It's over and finished. He's paid."

"Paid," exclaimed the younger man, black eyes showing quick fire. "They've killed him is what they've done, Bill. Ten years they give him for the shooting, sent him back after seven—and my gawd now I know why they sent him back to us. To die!"

Big Bill lifted his hat, scratched matted brown curly hair, dropped the hat back down and avoided his brother's glare when he said, "I told you—it's finished."

Jess hung there in breathless silence for a long moment. "Just—finished—because you say so?"

"No, because what in gawd's name good will it do to resurrect the thing, Jess? Seven years has gone by. Folks hardly even talk about it any more."

"But they will start talkin' about it again now," exclaimed the younger man. "Now he's back they'll bring it up again."

"Then it's going to be up to us to keep it from becoming anything more'n just towntalk. We won't get into any discussions about. It is finished. We're going to hold to that."

Jess continued to stare breathlessly at his larger and older brother. "Bill, for Chris'sake, he paid for what he done. All right; that part is paid off and finished. Did you ever figure they'd use him like that? Well—now tell me–don't that call for

11

some payin' back? Paw paid his dues, then they broke him down and don't you think someone owes them for that?"

Big Bill was not a man of completely endless patience. He was usually not irritable, but there was a limit and right now it had been just about reached. He glared. "Well; what you got in mind? They done it down at Yuma Prison. You expect to ride down there, ride around the walls pot-shooting at guards and all? Or maybe you figure to go and bushwhack the territorial governor?"

"I'll start with Blake Hobart and go on from there," exclaimed Jess icily, and leaned to hang his head in his hands. "It almost made me sick to see him get out of that buggy. I almost cried like a damned baby. But instead I didn't want him nor Blake to see, so I made a real hard face to them. . . . It just never crossed my mind . . . I figured like we talked last night; when he come back, all three of us would take up with the cattle and horses again like we was doing when they took him away. I just never figured he'd come back *like that.*"

Bill studied the scuffed, dusty toes of his boots with nothing more to add to what he had already said; a man lives his convictions, if they are deep and solid enough, regardless of the attacks of others upon them. He would not allow Jess to do any of the things he was irrationally talking about; things which justifiably, perhaps, sprang

12

from the cold and deep shock of seeing the old man when he climbed out of that top-buggy.

Beyond the clearing over against the dark-cloaked easterly sidehill which curved around to become another slope to the northward, a big cat screamed with its echoing cry following out the turn of the slopes.

Almost any other time they would have run for their guns. This was calving-time; those cougars haunted the secret slopes hidden among tree-shapes and dense underbrush. Nothing was more fatal to newborn calves.

Bill looked up, but Jess continued to sit, head in his hands. The cat was moving around the side-hill. They heard him sound again to the north-ward, but after that he was silent. In many ways they were more to be feared when they were still.

Bill arose, stepped to the door, reached around it and brought forth a saddlegun. He stood a while upon the porch-edge debating whether to saddle up, and behind him in the doorway the old man appeared and said, "You hear him, boys? Off to the left there above the calving-ground. There's not a heap of daylight left."

Bill turned, nodding his head. "Come along," he said to his brother. "Fetch your carbine and let's get over there."

Edson said, "I'll cook supper, have it ready when you get back. I expect the pelt won't be worth much, the weather getting warm now." He watched them troop off the porch in the direction of the old log barn.

There was plenty of daylight, and that was rarely an advantage under these circumstances, for while it might enable men to read fresh sign in the pine needles and the creek-crossings it also enabled a stealthy predator such as that big cat, to see horsemen along his back-trail, and the only way he had survived this long was by being extremely wary.

But these particular horsemen had hung their share of puma hides on the barn sidewall to cure. They did not continue on horseback after they were a mile and a half up there, around the forested slope, they left the horses tethered and went ahead soundlessly on foot.

The chances were excellent that they would not find this cougar. Not if he kept moving, but with the scent of fresh afterbirth rising from the calving-ground where the cows were herding close in the thin, good spring-air sunshine, there was a better than even chance he had not gone on.

The men did not speak, did not make a sound, did not step into a single sun-speckled clearing. They were accomplished at this sort of thing. They were, in fact, the two best stalkers in the countryside. If the old man had been that good seven years ago when he shot Weaver Johnson out of his saddle they never would have caught him like they did.

TWO
A Time of Memories

Daylight was out yonder in a deep, steady flow, but back through mottled forest-gloaming where Big Bill came to rest beside a tough-barked bull-pine unless there was movement it was almost impossible to separate shapes from shadows.

They were roughly where the cougar had been when he had screamed last. They had not tracked him—that took too long—but they knew these slopes, had known them from boyhood; if something wished to hide here, it could not possibly do it successfully if the Black men were stalking it, especially something as large as a big cat.

The cattle were terrified. Out, down through the trees Bill and Jess could see their dumb-brute consternation, old cows nuzzling spindly-legged calves up close, steers, with no real reason to remain anywhere, beginning to break out and trot off, heads high. The old redback bulls, two of them, coming around like ships in a rough trough, heads towards the uphill slope.

Among those redbacks there was no defense against a cougar, wicked horns notwithstanding, and even the old bulls standing heroically between the cows, calves and young stock, and that wooded slope seemed to know it.

Maybe they could discern the faint-distant scent

15

of men, although there was not a sigh of wind to carry it down there. Probably not, otherwise the big cat would have detected that scent too, and he was more likely to be expecting. In any event he was moving with the hush of a death-dealer, one yard at a time, great padded feet settling as gently as new-fallen snow with each downhill step he took.

He had the cattle well in sight, knew which baby calf was closest. He had not eaten in three days. That warm-meat smell was like a drug to his brain. He fatally did not once take his eyes off the wet cow and her baby calf.

He moved with a cinnamon-colored sinuousness, long, low body strung out close to the ground, great tail faintly curved near the four-foot tip, small head and dark muzzle thrust dead ahead parallel with sloping tawny shoulders. His last two hundred feet would be in the clear so he would have to run with lightning speed. He was ready for that.

Where he stopped, tail low and swishing, Jess breathed his words. "Big 'un. Male or female, can you make out?"

Bill did not respond until the cat was in stealthy movement again, then he whispered back, "Male."

They could not so much as raise a carbine yet. The cat could detect movement instantly even when it was behind him and off to his left. But even if he hadn't been able to, neither Bill nor Jess could risk a miss. Not with this one; he was old and vastly experienced and clever. Any movement now and he would whirl with tremendous speed and spring fifteen feet to land racing away.

They had to risk that calf, had to let the cougar get just close enough to the final fringe of forest so that he would not detect it when they settled low to one knee and aimed.

A jaybird landed clumsily above and saw the men. He immediately set up a fierce and agitated caterwauling hopping from skinny leg to skinny leg, screaming, ruffling, springing agitatedly here and there to scold and denounce. Jaybirds were the woodland sentinels; every wild animal heeded their raucous denunciations. The big cat, eyes fixed narrowly upon the baby calf, heard, and lashed with its tail, halted and lashed more furiously as the bird screamed its warning. He was clearly torn between taking heed and making his run.

Bill nudged Jess. They sank slowly, raised guns and snugged them back, and the bird increased its outraged screaming. At the very last moment something dim in the big cat's brain sounded the alarm; he tore clear of his staring southward and turned.

He saw the men. Bill fired. Jess was momentarily thrown off by that, and as the big cat sprang high and twisted to land facing away, Jess also fired. Bill was levering up his next load as the cat came down on all fours and briefly hung there. Then the red burst of blood gushed and he made no further attempt to see the men or to speed away. He hung there. Jess was ready again but Bill grounded his saddlegun watching.

The big cat did not weave, he simply folded all four legs on the way down as though he were composing himself for sleep.

Blood continued to gush.

Jess lowered the carbine, leaned down gazing over there, and only the dull beat of cloven hooves against spring-hard earth out at the calving-ground eventually pulled his glance away.

The cattle had been teetering upon the edge of running panic before the gunshots; now they were totally unnerved. But there were two thousand Black acres for them to run across and long before they got even close to the border with Johnson's Flesh-Knife outfit they would be run down.

Bill arose and walked ahead. The big cat's brilliant eyes were glazing, his body was emptied of blood and lying slack. Death, even of a mortal enemy, was somber to behold—unknowable.

Jess walked over too, Winchester hooked in the sling of a bent arm. "Old tom," he observed, then the same pain came over him too at this sight of death. They never spoke of it but both remembered with vivid clarity how it was that night with the storm-wind gusting that their mother had died. They were not new to death, even then.

They were not God-fearing; they had matured in the casual heathenism of the frontier wilderness. They had never known aught but the touch of adversity, the sternness of life or death, one or the other without an in-between of any kind. They believed in the seasons, in the sky-signs of weather change, in the black, warm earth of planting time, of the need to kill as they had just done without compunction or contemplation, and in this they did not differ from any neighbor, or most of the townsmen over at Frontera.

Still, to stand in calmness and view death opened great doors upon an unknowable darkness which made them question—but never doubt—their purpose, their reason, their rules and their wants.

Bill spoke, finally. "Let's haul him up to a tree-fork on the game trail."

Which was what they did, the reasoning being that other cats—and wolves and coyotes, most predators which might also be drawn to the calving-ground—would be warned off.

It worked every time.

Then they returned to the barn, put out the horses, saw smoke from the house-chimney and light from one of the two windows in the outer wall, and paused in the barn doorway to briefly gaze out through the settling late-day shadows.

Bill became busy with his carbine, head lowered when he said, "Jess, we hadn't ought to question him about how it was. No sense in that, for a while anyway."

"Yeah, I know. And act like he's only been gone a short spell and don't look any different. Bill, I'm a damned poor hypocrite."

Bill said, "You'll do," and walked on.

The old man had made cornbread gruel for supper with some of their precious bottled beef mixed in, and seasoned with sage. He looked up and listened when they told him about the cat, then noddingly went back to his stove-work perfectly satisfied. He had always told them death was more nearly present every moment of the day than sunshine, and it certainly seemed to most of the time.

They banked a fir-knot fire after supper and sat talking quietly with tin mugs of black coffee, Jess and Bill being very careful, listening mostly as the old man rambled on and on about how time had a way of telescoping into itself until seven years did not seem at times to have been more than two or maybe three years.

He spoke of their mother—he had once said he would be nothing without her and maybe now for a fact, it was true. He was nowhere near the man she had seen them poke up into the prison wagon. It was possible she was better off not seeing him as he now was.

Finally, he touched upon one topic they had ached over down the troubled and lonely years. The killing.

"I told your Maw, and she knew anyway, but since she never told you boys—too young for it back then I expect—well; it'd best be talked out now."

He refilled all cups from the old graniteware pot and resumed his seat across from them at the table.

"You know the Johnsons got five times the land we could file on when we first come out here. And you know they'd been here fifty years before us, had been usin' out filed-on land for late fall feed. . . ."

"And you and Weaver had a fight one time in town," said black-eyed Jess in a dull voice which sounded tired.

"Yes. Me without a pistol, only the rifle in the wagon. I still got scars from that pistol-barrel. It took your Maw three weeks to get me back up and able."

Edson cupped thin-veined hands around the tin cup for pleasant warmth.

"I owed him for that as God was my witness. I told Blake the day I was able to ride to town afterwards, the following month, I owed him for that pistol beatin' and Blake said I was lucky he hadn't shot me, gun or no gun, because he hated my guts and the guts of my whole brood for comin' in here and filing on his land."

Bill drank, pushed the cup clear and said, "Paw; we know all this. We've been hearin' it since they taken you away. Why don't we just all turn in now, you look tired and—."

"You listen," broke in the old man, a hint of his old oaken stubbornness briefly showing. He had been a strict parent, but always a fair one and, most of the time, also an understanding one.

"Boys, I figured you'd hear every detail and not once would you hear my side of it. So now you listen. I been thinking about this for seven, almost eight, years."

Bill subsided, mighty shoulders hunching lower across the table.

"I never rode out after that unarmed again . . . They were workin' it different. I didn't die from havin' half my skull stove in and my ribs kicked apart, so they started working on the cattle. I'd find one poisoned, another one shot, three head one time drove over a bluff six miles from here on Johnson range . . . Boys, I was one man. You was too young and besides it wasn't something lads nor women were supposed to even know about—evening things up.

"I rode the rims and watched, and when I knew how Weaver rode his summertime rounds I went out one night, got into some rocks, and come morning when I could see him coming alone, I lay the gun—that one, Jess, the one you use now—I lay it atop some rocks."

Jess looked up without raising his head. "Murder, Paw, pure and simple."

Edson raised a hand and smiled at his youngest. "Wait; I know what you've heard but just wait and let me finish. It was *not* murder, son. No sir and Gawd's my witness." The humorless smile lingered as the older man also said, "He don't help worth a damn in a courtroom.

"I let Weaver get right up close. He was wearing that ivory-handled Colt and his carbine was swung forward. You know folks don't carry carbines like that in rough country unless they figure they might want to use one, fast.

"I let him get up close enough, then I called him. I said, you son of a bitch, now try it when we're equals. He stopped the horse plumb flabbergasted. He could see my head over the rocks."

"What did he say, Paw?"

"Not a blessed word, Jess, he finally moved like lightning. He went down the far side of his horse with his right hand on the saddlehorn and his left hand going for that fancy six-gun. I shot him through the skull; blew the whole topmost part off. The horse commenced to rear and buck, shook him loose and run like the wind back the way they had come . . . You know the rest of it."

Jess had a question. "That gun with the ivory stock—did he draw it, Paw?"

"Gospel truth, Jess, he had it in his hand." The old man stared steadily at his youngest. "I know what they said at the trial—the gun was still in its holster when his riders got out there. I'd bushwhacked Weaver neat as a whistle, but it was not the truth. He had that gun in his hand, and when I walked down there it was still in his grip. Son, I called him. I give him a better chance than he gave me in Frontera, walking up behind me out front of the store and knocking me half dumb with his first pistol strike over the head . . . Jess, boy, it was exactly as I just now said it was. He died tryin'."

Bill gently worked his cup back and forth in its small sticky dark puddle. "Paw . . . it's time to turn in," he said quietly, a gentle giant with the old man's identical gun-metal gray eyes.

"Sure," replied the old man, and drained his cup, looked down at them and said, "I come straight home and told your mother. Then we waited, and she cried."

"And they come," mused Jess. "I've heard about that. You gave up to Blake only after he ran you down. Paw, why the hell did you go home, why didn't you ride for it right then?"

"Because your mother had to be told the truth."

Jess stared. The old man understood and then said, "Boy, don't pass a judgment until you too have a good woman, *then* come around and tell me I did wrong."

"She died, and you served seven years—and you could have outrun them."

24

"And if they'd overtaken me, Jess, and had killed me which was what they aimed to do— your mother would never have known that I hadn't murdered Weaver."

Jess screwed up his face. "It was that important?"

Big Bill arose. "It's late and I'm going to turn in. Good night, Paw. In the morning if you'd like we'll ride out in the wagon."

THREE
A Visit from the Law

Tige Johnson was a rawboned, rangy-built man of slightly over six feet who sat a horse like he'd been born up there, and who wore an ivory-stocked six-gun which had once belonged to his father.

He had known Edson Black was coming home, but that was the same day he had to take a top-rig and go down to rail's-end at Grantsville and get Bertha his widowed sister who was coming home, now, after six years of being married to a city-man over at Council Bluffs.

Nor had Tige made up his mind; he knew what he would *like* to do, knew what folks might even expect him to do—settle up a killing with a killing—but although he hated the Blacks with a full and unrelenting passion, what he hated them for had happened a long time ago. He had in fact been eighteen years old when his father had been killed, big enough by most standards but certainly not skilled enough to exact vengeance, and since those days he had been unable to think of much beyond the responsibility of his inheritance—the Flesh-knife cow outfit.

Nor had the Black brothers made trouble. They had never allowed their upgraded redbacks to cross onto Flesh-knife grassland, and they seemed to seek no confrontations either, on the range or in town with either Tige or his four riders.

But mostly, sinewy, tough Tige Johnson had never made up his mind. That day old Edson Black had returned, Blake Hobart had ridden out in the evening to sit on the porch with Tige and his widowed sister and quietly discuss things which had been bothering him lately, like the way blood-feuds perpetuated themselves, and how senseless killings to avenge other killings were, and throughout Blake's rambling, buxom, red-headed Bertha Johnson had sat mutely listening until her brother said, "Sheriff, I got nothing to say except that for seven years we've hardly more than seen one another. They stay on their side, we stay on our side. As for the old killer returning. . . ."

Bertha sighed. "How can folks excuse murder, Mister Hobart? They can't. But to me—it should be allowed to just go along, us living on our side, they living on their side." She met Blake Hobart's level look with a gaze just as level. "One more killing—and I don't believe it could ever stop again." She faced lanky Tige. "You won't, and they won't. . . . Maybe some time they'll load up and move on." She looked back at Sheriff Hobart. "Maybe. But whether that happens or not—don't warn us, Sheriff, unless you also warn them. Then let's just try and not keep the hatred forever."

Tige screwed down his face. He had the hatred inside as solid as steel. But at this moment he did not mention it. Instead he offered Sheriff Hobart a drink of rye whisky, and had to then arise and enter the lighted house at his back to get the bottle and glasses, and during his absence handsome Bertha said, "The bad part is living this close to one another."

Blake shook his head. "The bad part is what they did to Edson Black in prison. He is a dyin' man, and when he left here he was big and stout as a bull."

She looked enquiringly over. Blake shrugged. "Those two boys looked on him when I helped him down out of the buggy like they was stricken, like they couldn't believe what had been done to him. Ma'm, *that's* the bad part, especially with young Jess; he's fiery and fierce when he gets a bow in his neck."

"They wouldn't lay that to our door," said Bertha.

27

"Bill—no," responded Blake. "Jess—you never know with a man like Jess . . . It worries me."

Tige returned. For a while nothing more was said. Blake Hobart was a man who appreciated good whisky, and while it had seldom been claimed by makers of whisky that the rye variety was best—unless of course they exclusively manufactured it—tonight it mellowed the troubled sheriff, so much so in fact he cast a sidelong glance at the abundant and very handsome figure of the woman sitting between his chair and her brother's chair. Blake Hobart had been a widower for twelve years. That was a very long dry spell.

Tige brought the lawman's thoughts back to the situation they had been discussing when he said, "Seems to me things could go along as they have, Sheriff. What the hell—seven years and we still haven't got into a pitched battle, them and us. That proves something."

To Sheriff Hobart it indeed proved something; it proved that enemies could perhaps live within sight of each other indefinitely, providing they were reluctant or undecided. It proved that showdowns were not inevitable.

But the day Edson Black returned the old wound had been reopened whether anyone said so or not, and *this* was what had brought Blake Hobart out to the Flesh-knife this afternoon: It remained the paramount thought this early evening, with the faint first chill of a high-

28

country night close by while he sat sipping his rye whisky.

What worried him was that while nothing might erupt soon—maybe even not this year at all—without a single doubt, eventually there was going to be a meeting, something said, something *done.* Blake Hobart was not a man with many illusions left.

What, exactly, would come out of a face-down? Not particularly between Big Bill and Tige, but between Jess and Tige—or Jess and any of the Flesh-knife riders who were down across the yard tonight, behind the old log walls of that lighted bunkhouse.

Tige said, "Well, Sheriff, I rassled with this most of my grown life. You'd figure a man during all that time would have come up with a right answer."

Tige smiled at his handsome sister.

"I don't have enough killer-instinct in me," he told them both, but while looking directly at her. "I've said this before. I don't want to kill someone."

Blake pushed for something more definite than that. To force some kind of more definitive answer he said, "Not even if it was murder, Tige?"

It was noticeable even in the failing light when Tige flinched. Afterwards, he hung fire for so long his sister spoke first.

29

She had been married and gone during most of that trying time after the gundown, had only known the Blacks before that by distant sighting out over the range; whatever her sentiments, they could not possibly have the same depth of intensity as the feelings of her brother. Nonetheless she said, "Sheriff, I hope I'm wrong, but it seems to me that people are pushing my brother towards something he doesn't want to do." She looked squarely at Blake Hobart. He picked up the innuendo without effort and straightened slightly in his chair.

"Me?" he softly said.

She nodded, not the least bit daunted. "You and anyone else who keeps picking at this thing. Your purpose no doubt is sincere—how about the others down in Frontera, or for that matter around the ranges? And if this is being done to my brother—is it also being done to the Blacks? Sheriff; if it is, then people are going to force something which just simply does not have to happen."

Into the ensuing silence Bertha arose, took their empty glasses, the half-full bottle, turned and entered the house, letting the door swing softly closed at her back.

For ten seconds neither Blake Hobart nor Tige Johnson said a word or moved. Then the sheriff arose a little stiffly. "I'll see you around town," he coolly said, nodded and struck out down off the veranda towards the dark barn where his saddle animal had been stalled with the saddle loose and the bridle draped from the horn.

Tige Johnson sat watching the lawman's long stride, feeling angry, humiliated, and also embarrassed. This was a man's ranch, run and maintained and occupied by men until Bertha's arrival. Men had done the blunt speaking, when there had been a need for it, and Tige Johnson's word was the final pronouncement in all things. What his sister had just done—take the initiative in a conversation between men, then drop a blunt condemnation as though she had that right, was inexcusable.

After Blake Hobart rode out of the yard Tige arose to enter the house. He did not even get to the doorway; she was leaning there in the dusky gloom also watching that faint mounted shadow out yonder.

She said, "If you're angry, Tige, I'm sorry, but that's exactly what he was doing whether he realized it or not. He was trying to force you to say what you meant to do; was trying to force you to make a range-law kind of decision. And he won't be the only one, now that Mister Black is back."

Tige stood with big fists loosely clenched. "That's not your affair," he told her. "What we were talkin' about was man to man."

Her handsome large eyes swung to his face. "You are more than my brother, Tige, you are also all I have left of the men I have loved. I seem strong; you told me I was strong; it's not true, Tige, and one more death—I just can't do it again."

She whirled abruptly and fled deeper into the house leaving him half-understanding, and half-troubled, for her.

As the fierceness dwindled he turned back, but there was no longer any sign of the lawman, so he shifted his glance to the mighty log barn with its corral-network made of peeled fir poles out back, to the wagon-shed, the smokehouse, the cook-shack, the shoeing-shop, and finally the lighted log bunkhouse.

She had not really challenged his supremacy here. The most vital thing in his entire exis-tence—Flesh-knife, and his rule of it had not been threatened. Still and all whether folks believed in outspokenness in women or not, *he* didn't, and they were going to have to arrive at an understanding about that.

As for the other . . . He reached to open the door, go inside and head for his room. Tomorrow they had to begin making a gather for the marking-ground, and after that was finished with they had to start working the cattle. Beyond that there would be sifting out the late-calving cows to be taken north to the foothills, the steers, old bulls and dry cows to be sorted out and taken southward where they'd be handy for the autumn drive to rail's-end. . . .

He went to bed and slept like a baby, the way he had always managed to sleep because he worked himself as hard, often harder, then he worked his riders. Work and sweat and worry through unlimited hours were the price of ownership of an outfit as large and flourishing as Flesh-knife. Maybe, as Bertha privately thought, he had done this because it provided a perfectly respectable way to avoid thinking or acting, on that other matter. She had hoped hard he would go right on deferring the decision most men would have made long ago.

Now, after that visit from the Frontera lawman, she got ready for bed at the other end of the big old rambling log house beginning to discern a faint outline of someone's destiny. It made her a little sick to her stomach. She sat by candlelight upon the edge of her bed brushing her hair and looking at the shadowy image of her face in the wall-mirror, holding back the urge to tears—one more time.

Sleep helped, at least to the extent of giving everyone an eight-hour respite, but the issue remained. In fact, by early dawnlight it looked just as ominous as it had looked last night.

Tige and the crew had loped from the yard a half-hour earlier so she ate alone in the cookshack except for the sullen fat Indian woman named Buttercup who did the cooking, and she almost never spoke to the men, feigning lack of understanding, and while she had not said one word to Bertha either, those first weeks, now she was able to grunt a little, which Bertha assumed with good-natured tolerance was a beginning.

Except that this particular morning she would not have had anything to say back, if Buttercup had spoken. They were together in the big old room, Buttercup at the stove whittling turnips, carrots, potatoes into a huge stewpot, Bertha at the vacant long dining-table with her empty plate and her second cup of coffee—and her somber thoughts.

Later, she tried what had once worked very well when she needed distance and hush and natural beauty to winnow worry out, she went down to the corral, picked out a horse, rigged him, got astride and rode out in no special direction, just rode.

The land was vast, hilly to the east and somewhat hilly as well to the northward, but otherwise gently rolling, grassy and watered by a number of veiny little willow-lined crooked creeks which were evidently fed year round from the massif lying shadowly to the far north, visible, although many days ride away.

This was in most ways the best time of the year. At least for people whose livelihood came from the earth, grass and water, sunshine and browse. Everything was vigorously growing.

She encountered greasy fat cows with sassy

redback calves. She also saw several wapiti, but from a great distance. And the loose-stock was fanned out over along the northerly brakes and gullies, half secreted by irregular stands of trees, half mottled by sunshine filtered through high cloud-shapes.

All this her parents had marshaled, had worked into one rich holding. She remembered her mother fairly well but she remembered her father as though he had been alive yesterday. She had listened to his tales of how he had put Flesh-knife together. Why he had given it that strange name: Because he had originally hired out as a buffalo-skinner when he had arrived in the high-country. He had worked day and night to save enough money to start buying land and livestock. He had used the same fleshing-knife for three years; it had never chipped nor broken. He had often said it was that flesh-knife which had made the rest possible for him.

She remembered many things about him. He was hard and rough and uncompromising when he felt he had the right to be. He was notorious for his willingness to fight. He was also known for his fairness.

Her late husband had once said her father was of a breed the world was rapidly coming to have no real use for; that people were learning better ways to settle things than by knives, hatchets, rifles and carbines.

She had never argued with her husband, not even that time, but she had long ago learned to respect and admire hard men of resolute honesty like her father. She still admired them.

Tige, she told herself, loping overland with a light, pleasant springtime breeze in her thick mass of red hair, was not Weaver Johnson. But whether that boded good or ill she could not guess. All she wanted to be sure of right now, as she came down along the eastward wooded slopes, was that her brother would not kill the Blacks and they would not kill him.

Maybe, then, it was better that Tige was as he was—clearly indecisive about this one issue.

FOUR
A Meeting

She entered a tier of tall trees along the base of a crooked slope and poked on through out of mid-morning sunlight until pine-sap-fragrance which was combining with the depth of sweet shade to create a wonderful private environment, took her into its depths and let her ride a loose rein, relaxed, and worrying far less than she had been worrying back at Flesh-knife.

She knew death. She knew suffering. She also knew beauty, and what a woman's love for a particular man could be—consuming, overpowering, breathtaking for months on end—even for years.

She had lived more, in less time, than her brother had, but their worlds had diverged when she met her late husband and had gone out of the high-country into the world of flounces, parasols and pearl-grey derbies on handsome pink-faced men. She had never expected to return, certainly not as she had—widowed.

The pain was atrophying but it had taken a long while. She knew about showing one face to the world and another to her pillow. She knew about desolation, and crying, until there was not a single tear left.

From these many crucibles she had emerged looking just as abundantly handsome as before, just as redheaded-green-eyed-buxom-beautiful, but that was the outside; inside she had emerged as strong as steel, as deep as a mountain lake, as understanding and perceptive as any woman who had ever lived.

But her sense of direction was not the best. She rode right up onto the kneeling man without having any idea there could be another human being within miles. Her horse was soundless over the centuries-old, springy ground-covering of pine needles. The man, though, detected the sound of leather over leather, the slight sound of metal parts. He came up and around in a whirling movement which made her half-asleep horse abruptly plant all four legs stiffly down and nearly propel her over the saddlehorn.

He was a large man with eyes the shade of gun-metal, and although his face was slightly angular, the features were good, the jawbone iron-like, the chin and mouth uncompromising.

She was certain of just one thing; he was not a Flesh-knife rider, and therefore he was tres-passing on Flesh-knife land, which was no inex-cusable offense, actually, even though her brother had never encouraged trespassers.

She recovered, sat back, considered the pow-erful chest, shoulders, arms, and the big scarred dark hands.

He said, "Good morning. You gave me a start." He did not smile as he studied her. "You'd be from Frontera, maybe, and rode out a mite farther than you figured?"

"I came from . . ." She saw the bundle at his feet. "What were you doing here?"

He looked down. "Killed a big cat not far from here a few days back, and last night we lost a calf so I came out here to make this ambush." He nudged the furry bundle with a big boot. "There's a trap under this remnant of the dead calf." He looked up at her, still wanting to explain, acting as though she were a child, or someone who at least was uninitiated. "They commonly travel in pairs. We killed the male cat—the tom."

She sat listening, fitting some pieces of a half-remembered mosaic together in her mind. She knew who he was. At least she had deduced that he was *one* of them. She had no idea which one, nor did it matter right at this moment. She turned, looking to her left, trying to recall exactly where the boundary-line was. She looked back as she said, "Are you on Flesh-knife?"

He shook his head. "No, ma'm. This here is Black land. From here east to that fir snag you can see up the easterly slope, and from there southward. There's a meadow and a house down yonder." He lifted his dark gray eyes. "I'm Bill Black."

Her reaction was, in theory at least, supposed to incline her to also make an introduction. She might have, too, except that from the middle distance southeasterly through the trees a man sang out.

"Where'd you get to, Bill?"

The large man turned with an easy grace usually foreign to people his size, and called back. "Up through here, Jess. Follow the tracks!"

She was turning her horse when he faced her again. She said, "Good day, Mister Black," and allowing him no chance to delay her, she started back down through the trees in the direction from which she had come.

It was several miles from Flesh-knife's yard to the Black rangeland, she did not remember how many miles because she had been a youngster the last time she had ridden over here, but she realized now that she'd covered about three times as much countryside as she had expected to cross over.

She knew she had seen Bill Black before, also, but right at this moment she could not recall the occasion. Perhaps on the range as a youngster, or maybe over in Frontera on a Saturday when most folks arrived from the countryside with wagons or pack animals to carry off the week-end purchases.

She did not remember that he was that large, that tall and oakenly thickset. On the slow ride back she reflected upon what she had seen in his face, set it up against what Blake Hobart had said last night about Bill Black being less quick-tempered than Jess was, and she decided Blake had been correct. Bill did not have the aquiline cast of features which seemed to go with a temper, with lack of patience or tolerance. He was, the more she thought back, a nice-looking, pleasant-faced individual, without being handsome.

She made it into the yard and off-saddled while there was still a high, warming afternoon sun, and trooped across to the cookshack for company because there was not another soul, other than Buttercup, on the place. Last night her brother had mumbled something about making a gather. . . .

Buttercup had her squat bulk at the table with a cup of hot coffee and glanced up with stony disenchantment as Bertha entered the long, cool old room. Buttercup pointed to the coffeepot.

Bertha smiled, brought her full cup to the table opposite the other woman, sat and said, "I got lost. Rode too far east."

Buttercup's muddy dark eyes rested upon Bertha's face. "You get to Black range?"

It was almost the longest single sentence Buttercup had spoken since Bertha's arrival at Flesh-knife. Clearly, it had solid concern behind it, too. "You don't go over there. You stay west or north or south. Don't go over there!"

Bertha pretended not to be surprised at both the length of Buttercup's pronouncement, and the vehemence of it. She sipped coffee, met the Indian woman's stare and said, "Wasn't that a long while ago?"

Buttercup would not argue. "Don't go on Black range! *Dina sica!*"

Bertha shrugged and smiled. "I value your friendship," she said quietly, holding the muddy dark eyes with her gaze. "I'll be careful . . . But— that was a long time ago."

"People no good," exclaimed Buttercup, clearly letting something out which had been pent up a long time; maybe years, "who don't take blood for blood. There will be bad punishment on people who don't get revenge!"

Bertha's smile faded. She arose to go refill the cup at the stove and to turn back solemnly. "Buttercup, in all the years since then the ranch has prospered, my brother has earned respect—

41

what good would it be to anyone at all if they killed him or if he killed them?"

The squat dark woman turned a little so she could meet Bertha's glance. "You like murder? You think it's all right to live like this and your father is being tortured in his grave?"

It would be a losing argument no matter whether they kept it alive for a year or more. Bertha considered the brew in her crockery cup. They not only came from totally divergent environments, they were also different in their convictions.

She finally said, "Could we just be friends, Buttercup? We are the only women."

The Indian woman did not say a word, she heaved up to her feet taking the cup with her back to the stove where she lifted a lid and using a long-handled wooden spoon, stirred, her broad back planted indignantly in front of Bertha Johnson, so erect that her posture alone spoke volumes.

Bertha returned to the yard.

The men were trickling in, two from the southward range, her brother and his rangeboss Claude Freeman, with another rider, from the heat-blurred west.

She did not go over and await their arrival. She had learned a lesson about *that*. Men who ordinarily swore very little, were different at day's end when they were tired. She went to the veranda, sat up there until Tige finished at the barn and trudged homeward without seeing her until he was close to the steps. Then he looked up.

She smiled. "Long day?"

He looked tiredly back. "They're all long. You went riding?"

That surprised her until he trooped on up, dropped his hat beside a chair and sank into it. "Saw a sweat-backed horse in the corral. Where did you go?"

"Around," she said evasively.

He was not very interested, which was just as well. She did not need another admonition. He said, "I haven't been culling hard enough the past few years. We got far too many barren old gummer cows this spring."

Being dissatisfied with himself made him mention something else. He had never brought this up around her before. In fact, he almost never discussed the ranch with her. He was like their father in this, and some few other ways.

"Claude figured it out to be that folks have used up the first and best nutrients of the soil over the past fifty years . . . The grass even in a good year like this is, just isn't comin' on like it always has up to now . . . Over-grazing, Bertha." He turned as though this should shock her. It didn't. "I been holding back the pick of the heifer crop each year and ain't been—"

"*Haven't* been!"

43

". . . and *haven't* been culling out enough of the older cows. We're runnin' out of grassland. I never believed it could happen but Claude's right, now that I think back about it. I used to think it was lack of good, warm spring rains. Only we been getting those growing rains and Flesh-knife is still runnin' out of grass too early each autumn. You understand?"

She understood; it would have required no vast intellectual prowess to understand. He made it clear enough. She just could not get as worried as he seemed to.

"What is the answer?" she asked him.

He responded as though even an idiot would have discerned the solution. "More land, what else could the answer be? Flesh-knife's got to expand."

She said, "Can you do that, Tige?"

He slumped deeper into his chair. The shadows were coming more heavily now. Buttercup stepped out upon the porch and swung her steel rod inside the summoning triangle. Men erupted from the bunkhouse and went swiftly in the direction of supper.

Tige watched them, and only remembered his sister's question when the door slammed behind the rangeboss, last of the riding crew to cross over.

"It's something that's got to be thought over pretty careful," he told her. "Maybe I could drive north into the foothills farther. Maybe I could put a line camp up on the high meadows of the lower mountains. There's good grass up there."

She remembered something from childhood and mentioned it now. "Bear and wolves and cougars up there, Tige . . . ?"

He knew the source of her concern; their father. "That was a long while back," he retorted, then also showed his natural caution by saying, "but I'd keep men up there riding all season just the same."

It was free-graze. Any unused and unclaimed land was free-graze. But the time had arrived when good free-graze land was becoming very scarce. Mostly, if it existed at all, it did so only in places such as the mountain plateaus or big meadow-benches such as the territory Tige was discussing now, which had serious drawbacks. Aside from predators, the higher cattle were driven the shorter was the browsing and grazing season.

This worried Tige now, too. "I got to have about four months and maybe five. I'm not sure the snow'll hang off up there for that long."

For Bertha the practical side of any problem was the only side, so she said, "You wouldn't have to go up there would you?"

"No," he said softly. "No, I could expand over into the easterly and maybe the lower-down northerly mountains. There's grass in there, in parks and places."

She saw his shadowed profile turn solemn, and if she hadn't been into that same country this very day she might not have understood what he had in the back of his mind. She said, "Tige . . . ? The Blacks run cattle over there."

"It's not their land. Most of it up in there is free-graze." He shifted in the chair, sedulously avoiding her gaze.

"Tige . . . please don't. There are other ways open to you, I'm sure. Westward, perhaps, or even southward?"

"Taken up land, Sis, every mile of it. To pay cash money for it they'd likely want as much as half dollar an acre, which is just ridiculous."

"The mountains then."

He shrugged, considered the subdued noise over at the cookshack, then said, "Have you eaten?"

She hadn't, except for that coffee earlier, but she was not hungry. He was, so he arose, leaving his hat upon the floor beside the empty chair and struck out across the dusk-mantled yard.

She watched his progress, felt uncomfortable, and decided to insinuate herself more and more into ranch business. Flesh-knife belonged to him. She was perfectly willing to accept this feudal type of inheritance—handing it down from father to son, but as she had told him before, he was all she had left. She was going to take a vital interest whether Tige liked it or not.

46

For a while she sat in the cooling evening thinking of that other man she had encountered today, the big one called Bill.

Analyzing her feelings proved impossible. She had liked most of what she had seen of him, and yet in her subconscious mind was the full knowledge that he was the son of the man who had killed her father.

In fairness, of course, Bill could not be held responsible. Nor had he looked like the kind of an individual who would approve of killing any more than she did. On the other hand, she was guessing; basing a judgment upon the flimsiest of visual evidence.

She remembered the set of his chin and mouth . . . If Tige expanded into those foothills over there. . . .

She arose and went indoors, it was turning cold finally.

FIVE
A Woman

Claude Freeman the Flesh-knife rangeboss was more than a seasoned cowman and range supervisor, he was also an individual of considerable sagacity.

If he had shortcomings they evidently had little or nothing to do with his work because Tige hadn't had occasion to disapprove of anything he had done since hiring him years back.

He was older by quite a lot than the man who employed him, and yet they worked together as though there was no age-difference, and in fact Claude was the same way with the other riders, all younger than he was.

To Bertha Johnson he was a reliable, dependable rangeboss. Whatever he thought of her was masked behind a somewhat casual, somewhat formal method of address. Nor could she ever read much in his expression. That too, was under his perfect control, evidently.

The day she mentioned what her brother had said about expanding, they were together out back at the working-corrals where Tige and another man were trying to ease a troubled cow into the chute to doctor infected grub holes in her back. The cow had been inside that chute before; she planted her feet, switched her tail and was not going to be budged, until they got a lasso rope under her tail and upon two fir posts set three feet into the stone-hard ground just for this eventuality, then warped her ahead a foot at a time.

Claude was leaning beside Bertha on the outside watching. He shook his head and said, "Doggoned old critter; she knows she's going to get doctored. She's old enough to have been through there a dozen times."

Bertha saw her opening. "Does she have any teeth left?"

Claude studied the cow for a while then

answered evasively. "Likely not, but they'll fool you sometimes."

"Then why not cull her out?" asked Bertha, and the foreman turned to briefly gaze at her. He acted as though he had not been conscious of her before that question.

"Well; that'd be up to Tige, ma'am, but even so she's still got maybe five, six calves in her."

Bertha had more of an answer than she had asked for. She also had the answer as to why Flesh-knife had been keeping back so many head of she-stock. Claude Freeman believed in expansion. She was not sure her brother believed in it, even after listening to him last night, but even so, if he didn't, he would be a very unusual cowman.

She watched them slam the chute-gate and climb upon the catwalk in order to be able to safely lean down and go to work on the old cow's back.

Outside, the rangeboss finally straightened up, pulled gloves from beneath his shellbelt and looked pensively around at her as he pulled them on. Then he smiled and walked away.

She thought she had detected a change towards her in him. Not exactly hostility, not even noticeable antagonism, but something different from before, and it had not seemed to her to be favorable.

And yet the very next day when she went down to snake out a mount to ride forth upon, he was there at the gate with a rope and even selected the best horse for her, led it inside and gallantly rigged it out. Most of that time, while he said very little, he was smiling.

She rode to the easterly forested hills without really thinking very much about a destination. It was as though the easterly range and its forested boundary was a lodestone. She had been curious about that cougar-trap. At Flesh-knife they rarely tried to trap predators, they ambushed them with Winchesters.

The trap was gone. So was the remnant of calf-hide, but she rode half a mile farther up-slope and saw that success had crowned Bill Black's efforts; the limp tawny carcass of a female puma was draped from the crotch of a tree. She felt pain over the animal's death and revulsion at the barbaric method the Blacks used in disposing of the body. Indians would have done it like that but the Blacks were not Indians.

She turned down off the hill and angled in the direction of the Frontera road—which was actually an ancient set of work-deep ruts. Evidently a stage or some large vehicle had passed through not too long before because she could still smell dust.

There was a horseman angling far back towards the roadway, and evidently he had crossed the range where the Blacks ran their small herd because his route seemed to be diagonally onto

Flesh-knife towards the coachroad. Otherwise she saw no one for more than an hour, then she spied three loping riders, clearly rangemen even though they were too distant to make out much but their style of riding for some time after she first saw them.

They hauled down to a walk at sight of her. In fact they pulled down to a very slow walk, which was unusual for rangemen. She understood. She had not matured into an abundant, solid woman, lovely to look at, without realizing how men viewed her. It had never made her the least bit self-conscious, nor had it augmented her self-respect until it turned into conceit.

When those leaned-down, bronzed horsemen boldly smiled, and one touched the brim of his stained old graceful hat, she nodded back showing just enough small friendly smile without showing any more.

They passed. For a long while, almost until those three men crossed paths with the solitary rider farther back, they did not resume their gallop. Finally though they did. She turned once to glance after them and saw the solitary rider loping steadily towards her but without seeming at all interested in the fact that a beautiful woman was riding towards town as he was also doing.

She had been gone many years, the land had not changed but a good many of its residents had, and because of that she neither made an effort to identify the on-coming horseman nor to feel very interested or curious about him.

Not until she could hear the loose, easy lope steadily coming on behind her and twisted for a final look. Bill Black! She would have known his size anywhere, and now he was close enough for her to also see his angular, sun-ruddied features.

He recognized her, may in fact have done that long before they were within speaking distance. At any rate he slowed to a walk at her side as he said, "Good morning. The lady from Frontera again."

She cocked an eye at him but made no immediate effort to correct his error. "Beautiful day," she said.

He looked around and back. "Yes'm. Well, I've got to get up to town." As he lifted a reinhand he also said, "My Paw came down bad off some time in the night. We need a doctor for him pretty bad."

"How—sick?" she asked.

He considered the poised reinhand before answering. "I don't exactly know, but he don't seem to be able to move on one side very well."

She let her breath out slowly and remembered from years back watching this same thing happen to her husband's father, back in Nebraska. "Is someone with him?" she asked.

"My brother Jess, but—".

"Can he talk? Can your father talk?"

"Don't seem to be able to do it very well, ma'm." The poised reinhand settled slightly as Big Bill Black leaned slightly to signal his large mount to lope out again. "Proud to have seen you again," he told her and rode away.

She drew rein, watched him grow small on the Frontera road, made up her mind with typical resolution, turned back and booted out her chestnut gelding back the way she had come.

They died of strokes of course, but not usually for some time, and it was clear that neither Bill nor his brother had understood the nature of this affliction which had brought their father down.

She understood enough about it to know what should be done for the old man before the doctor got down there—*if* he got down there; she had been hearing unpleasant mumblings about the Frontera medical practitioner and his reluctance to drive out over the range country.

Where she had left the road earlier she was tempted to leave it again, but *he* had clearly come by a more direct route, so she slackened gait and went more slowly along until she found the place where he had come overland. There, she turned southeasterly and loped overland tracing out his tracks into a grassy large glen which had those forested slopes to the east and also to the north.

The log house was almost squarely in the middle of the meadow. There was a lazy spiral of smoke lifting into a clear, winy day from a stone chimney, and beyond the house were several small log outbuildings, and a well-made log barn.

She tried to recall this place from childhood and failed although she was positive she must have ridden over through here with her brother as a child. But buildings to children were simply buildings; things to be seen and forgotten.

Except for that twisting smoke there was no sign of life. She tied up at the rack across in the direction of the barn, turned and strongly strode to the porch. Evidently her solid footfalls brought him, but at any rate a dark-eyed, solid big man with an Indian's black gaze and lank coarse black hair opened the door and looked out at her as though she were an apparition.

"I met your brother on the road to town," she explained "I think I can help."

He would have stepped back but she shouldered past and as he gave ground he softly frowned. Then he closed the door.

The house was stone silent. She turned, pulling off riding gloves. "Where is he?"

Jess pointed to an ajar door across the dingy parlor. He watched her cross over and enter his father's room with an assurance, with a boldness he had never before encountered in a woman, but then Jess had only really known one woman in his life and he had not been able to know her for very long because his mother even in her best years had been part of a struggling kinship with her man.

Bertha had to wait briefly for her eyes to adjust; the room was naturally gloomy and to enhance that condition someone had nailed a blanket over the small back-wall window. She stepped ahead and hoisted the blanket aside, pegged it that way and turned back towards the still, emaciated man upon the old bunk-bed.

Jess came to the door looking angry because she had let light in. She saw this and was undaunted by it. "No one ever died of sunlight through a window," she told him, stepping to bed-side and leaning to look at Edson Black.

The sign of death was clearly upon him. She straightened back and without looking at Jess she gave him an order. "Fetch me some clean rags and a fresh sleeping gown for him—and some soap and water."

Jess could not believe it. She had walked in— *marched* in actually—had brushed him aside as though he were a child. Now she was giving orders and he had never before laid eyes on her in his life.

When he did not move she faced him, still in a bent-over posture, the fullness of heavy breasts forcing a strain upon the cloth of her dress, the clean round sweep of a strong thigh equally as noticeable.

Her green eyes were fixed upon Jess's black eyes. Her wealth of red hair showed dull rust in the slanting sunshine. Jess yielded a little at a time. She took him to her in an alliance as she had done with other people, other times. He went softly walking back across the parlor.

Old Edson was stricken, was stunned and struggling deep-down against showing any of the fear he felt. He could not hold a thought nor create a new one. He thought by instinct and this told him he was looking into the face of dark death—then someone pulled aside the blanket and sunlight came rushing.

He felt her wipe spittle from his mouth, felt her washing his face with warm, clean water, could not quite focus on her but knew she was not either of his sons.

She got Jess to help and they cleaned him, got a fresh nightdress on him—with considerable effort—and the odd feeling he had of flowing warm water inside his body somewhere, actually very near to *hot* water, distracted his awareness. But at best his mind drifted in and out of consciousness without him ever actually losing it. He knew he had been disastrously brought low because he could not move the way his body had been made to move. He was not immobile, he just simply could not make a coordinated movement. It baffled him more even than it frightened him. He had been a strong man most of his life.

The red-headed buxom woman brought in a chair and sat at bedside. Jess brought her coffee—twice. The last time Jess came and sat with her keeping a soundless vigil.

When she finally arose to walk back through the parlor Jess leaned, touched his father's hand and softly said, "Ride it out, Paw."

Then he went out to the woman in the parlor. She was pulling back old curtains, pushing aside things which obstructed sunlight. The parlor became as he suddenly could recall it being when he'd been a youngster.

She turned, sunshine streaming at her back, and said, "I saw it this way once in Nebraska. It's not the killing kind of stroke. This time. If it had been he wouldn't be able to focus his eyes. In fact he would be totally unconscious now—and maybe his face would turn nearly scarlet the way it did with my father-in-law back in Nebraska—after his second stroke. But, Jess—he will be an invalid for the rest of his life. To some extent anyway."

The burly, dark-eyed man continued to study her with level concern. Clearly, she was something he could not quite comprehend. She was vital and glowing. She made him feel uncomfortable and something else which he could not define—inadequate, maybe, or awkward. Every time she moved she did something which brought back something of a shredded memory to him of that other woman who had whisked in and out of this same room, this same house.

Except that this woman was younger.

She went to the stove, sniffed, looked at him in amused tolerance, rolled back sleeves to show strong arms, and went to work. She ordered Jess to do this and that, and he did it. He did not open his mouth except once when she cocked her head, then he strode powerfully to the door and flung it open.

"Bill's back," he exclaimed, and disappeared around the corner of the house.

SIX
Frontera and Back

The doctor from Frontera did not arrive that day. He had been out of town when Bill had sought his residence up there. Blake Hobart had promised to send the doctor down to the Black place the moment he arrived back in town.

Blake's word was good, but the doctor's top-buggy did not hove into the yard until the third day and by then Bill and Jess had pretty well made up their minds, with the help of the red-headed woman, that their father's stroke was not going to prove fatal.

This time.

The woman returned each morning, put them to work cleaning, changing things, bringing a warm, comfortable atmosphere to the house and the last time, the same day the doctor finally got down there, she sat for two hours with their father arguing without opening her mouth. She wrote things on a slate, then helped hold him while he wrote angry answers with the one arm and hand which would work. He had difficulty speaking; at least he had difficulty making himself understood, but if there were brain damage, as the medical practitioner said after an hour-long painstaking examination, it was not yet discernible.

Then the red-headed woman departed and when Bill and Jess went in to sit with the old man, and asked him why he and the woman had argued, he refused to write for them, would simply glare and although they held him up and placed the slate just so, he would only shake his head at them.

She did not return.

Two days later when her brother had to go up to Frontera she rode along with him in the rig. It was a lovely day, the air was sparkling clear, the road was uncluttered, they had a lively pair of animals on the tongue and her brother was in good enough spirits for her to suddenly tell him where she had been going the past few days, how she had met Bill Black on the road, and all the rest of it.

He drove staring at her. Then he flicked the lines and said, "Let the old son of a bitch die, can't you?"

She was not shocked nor irritated. "Yes, I can do that, but I can't *kill* him, Tige, and that's what it would amount to because this was not a fatal stroke . . . Tige?"

"What!"

"He can't talk but he can write fairly well with one hand."

"What of it?"

"He told me about that shooting."

"Well; he told about it at the trial too, and before, while he was in the jailhouse." Tige gripped the loose lines with white knuckled hands. "Bertha, just leave it be, can't you? You're as bad as Blake and Claude and some others. I got along this well for this long just by leaving it be. Why do you of all folks have to start it up again? Last month when Blake come down to talk you said—."

"Tige," she broke in spiritedly, "I'm not trying to stir it up. Mister Edson asked me—would he have another stroke. I told him to ask the doctor, that I was just a person who had done for another man his age what I'd done for him. Then he asked me my name and when I wrote it on the slate he got excited, motioned for me to help him, and he wrote something back to me, on the slate."

"Bertha, confound it," exclaimed Tige.

"Just let me finish."

"Bertha, that's the man killed our Paw, and

60

there you was doctoring the old bastard and helpin' to keep him—."

"I said—damn it, Tige—*let me finish!*"

He drove on sitting hunched forward, profile showing a locked-down jaw and an iron-set mouth. She leaned to lightly place a hand upon his arm, very gently. She squeezed as though to say she was sorry for a flash of temper, then she said, "He wrote on the slate . . . Tige, do you remember a man named Bart Flack?"

"Sure. Rangeboss on Flesh-knife when we was kids."

"*Were* kids . . . Yes, that's who he was. Do you remember very much about him?"

Tige shrugged. "Big feller, rode out with Paw a lot, made a good partner for Paw, I heard Maw say one time. That's all. What of it?" He turned to look at her.

"One of the things Mister Black wrote was that Bart had to be the man who put Paw's pistol back in the holster after the killing. He wrote on the slate that Bart was the first one out there, and it had to be him who made that gundown look like a murder."

Tige shrugged again. "You're never going to get Bart Flack to tell you."

"Why not? The law can get out a summons."

"Because he's dead, that's why not, Sis. Flack was killed at Raton over in New Mexico Territory three years back. I hired some fellers to help on a drive to rail's-end couple years ago who knew about that."

Tige turned a long look upon Bertha, then clucked up the team because town was in sight ahead and he wanted to get back home before nightfall this same day.

Bertha braced when the horses hit their collars. After that the rattle and bounce made talking difficult. Nor did she know what, exactly, to say.

Her private feeling was that old Edson Black had not lied, because he knew he was close to death. Maybe she was attributing a sense of urgency and honesty to him which he did not actually possess, but it was difficult to believe that anyone, in the face of death, would willingly die with a lie on their lips and in their hearts.

Finally, on the outskirts of Frontera, she leaned towards her brother as he pulled the hitch down to a jog, and said, "Who was with Bart out there, that day?"

Tige pursed his lips in an expression of disapproval. "Bertha, just leave the damned thing be, can't you?" he exclaimed, and swerved to avoid a foot-deep chuck-hole.

Blake Hobart saw them pass in the roadway over near the jailhouse where he was in conversation with two faded cowmen. He got clear at once and hastened to the tie-rack out front of the general store where Tige was looping the shank. Blake offered Bertha a hand down, which she accepted more to impress upon her brother how such things should be done than because she needed help alighting.

Tige was a trifle curt with the lawman. He nodded, spoke briefly, and hastened on into the store. If Blake Hobart noticed it did not appear to bother him. He held Bertha's hand to the side-walk then she gently freed herself as he said, "I heard from Doc Spencer that Ed Black had a stroke, so maybe things will take care of them-selves after all."

She was annoyed by that so as she spoke she cocked a skeptical eye at the sheriff. "Take care of themselves?"

"Well, if the old man dies that won't leave the sons with a livin' reminder, will it?"

The logic was specious at best. She tried not to show feeling as she responded. "I don't believe Mister Black was ever a danger to us."

"Yeah. Just to your Paw," droned the lawman softly.

She could not quite force a smile so she said, "Thanks for helping me down," and turned to go after Tige in the general store.

Blake stood rooted and thoughtful until a bearded, dark man strolled up, discreetly spat aside, turned back and quietly said, "That there is one hell of a woman, Blake."

Sheriff Hobart nodded without saying a word, then he too turned away.

An hour later while she was outside the abstract office waiting for Tige, she saw the doctor approaching and caught him just short of the saloon. He smiled a little dubiously.

When she asked about Edson Black, he turned that aside and said, "Will you explain to me, young lady, why you didn't tell them who you were?" He sniffed, then tucked two fingers into a vest pocket as he stared at her. "That put me in a bad light. They told me about you and said you was a lady from Frontera. I knew better from the description. Will you explain that to me?"

"Doctor, I went over there to help a sick man. That's all. What possible good would it do to tell them I was Tige Johnson's sister? Besides, if they were all that interested, their father could have told them."

"He knew?"

"No, not until I told him."

The doctor pondered this, then loosened in his attitude a little. "By now no doubt he's enlightened them. Well; all right; as far as I'm concerned it's settled. And just maybe you was right at that. What would be the point in telling them—they likely wouldn't have allowed you near their Paw."

"How is he, Doctor?"

The older man still had his fingers tucked into a vest pocket when he squinted shrewdly at her. "You can guess. You have been through that

64

before. I can surmise that without trouble. How is he? The Lord could answer that, except that he won't. Edson Black could live another five, six years. Maybe even longer. Or he could have another stroke next week, eh?"

"Is there anything more I could do for him, Doctor?"

". . . You baffle me. That is the man who shot your Paw."

She had become sensitive about having people make this remark. "Doctor, I didn't say I approved of him, did I? He's a suffering human being."

The older man thinly smiled. "All right. No, there is little anyone can do for him except wait and see how much damage has been done to the brain, the nervous system, the muscles and so forth, then try to help him where he needs it most." He continued to stand gazing at her for a moment, then he spoke again.

"You did enough. You cleaned up that rathole and let in some light and made them keep the windows open. I've been out there down the years a few times—it was like going into a boar's nest." He cast a long look in the direction of the saloon, bowed slightly, stepped around her and continued on his way.

He was not a person who projected an image of compassion, nor was he a man people instinctively admired. On the other hand he was a good doctor; at least he was much better than the second choice around the Frontera countryside. The second choice was a man named Alberston who was also the undertaker. He had never completed any schooling and his actual practice of medicine had been largely limited to horses and cattle. But there were still a few utterly ignorant individuals who preferred Alberston to the regular physician.

Bertha saw her brother coming and walked back to the rig, climbed in and was sitting patiently when he freed the team, backed it clear, climbed in and turned back southward out of town, wearing a little scowl. She let him get well away before asking about the frown.

"The land south and west can't be bought nor leased," he announced. "That's what we come up here to find out about today." He thumbed back his hat, settled against the rear cushion and allowed the team to pick its own gait down the stageroad. He was displeased, patently, so when she picked up the conversation again she was discreet enough to approach things indirectly.

"There are the highland meadows and parks, Tige, and besides that it's been wet enough this spring to guarantee feed into autumn, hasn't it?"

He looked at her. "Wet enough—yeah—but I already explained to you, Bertha, it's not the quality of the feed it's the quantity of it. We got to expand our land holdings."

"Or cull closer, Tige?"

His eyes flashed. He started to sharply rebuke her, hung fire until the moment of heat passed, then he leaned ahead to look on down the countryside in the direction of the place where they would swing off the road.

Out of a clear blue sky he said, "Bertha, are you figuring on getting married again?"

She was surprised, of course, but intuition told her why he had asked that. He was resentful of her interest in Flesh-knife. Not because he felt she was a threat of any kind, but because she was a woman.

She neither answered him nor spoke again until long after they had abandoned the roadway and were bouncing along over Flesh-knife's northerly rolling low grassland-range. And even then she said nothing until he struck up a fresh conversation while squinting off towards the distant opening in the easterly hills where the Black outfit was.

"Feller at the abstract office figures the Blacks might want to sell out if the old man dies."

"The doctor was not hopeful about his dying, Tige," she told him. "He said Mister Black might even live another five or six years."

Tige sat forward, whipped up the team and they went bouncing headlong down towards the ranch-yard.

Dusk arrived before they got all the way back,

which was better than either of them had expected for this long day. They put up the team with bright lights showing from the cookshack where the men were at supper.

Tige stood in the front barn opening afterwards, mopping the sweatband inside his hat and looking preoccupied about something. When she came up to pause at his side he looked around at her.

"Do you figure to go on lookin' out for that old son of a—."

"Tige Johnson that is *not* necessary!" she flared at him and stepped past briskly on her way towards the distant mainhouse.

He swore heartily under his breath and hurried after her. They reached the wide low veranda steps at the same time. He caught her arm.

"Sis; I'll start over. Do you figure to go on helping *Mister* Edson Black?"

She glared at him. "Why? What's your interest?"

"Well, I been thinking that if you was to go back over there . . . They must like you to let you inside the house to look after him and all . . . I been thinking that you could find out if, when the old man dies, they will be selling out."

She looked at him in something close to speech-less anger, then turned and marched into the house, slamming the door after herself.

He looked up there, lifted his hat, scratched, dropped the hat down and turned in monumental disgust heading across towards the cookshack.

SEVEN
Mixed Feelings

Claude Freeman and two Flesh-knife riders, a man named Clinton Anderson and another man named Jett Smith, had already started the split-off the day Tige and his sister drove up to Frontera. They in fact had a big handle upon the entire project by the following day when Tige rode down to see what had been accomplished.

They had gummer cows, barren cows, old blank-shooting bulls and some hold-over steers which had been too light last year and which were heavier this year than Flesh-knife usually had its steer-end when it was peeled off and drifted to rail's-end.

It was, as Claude told Tige, a motley gather of cull cattle, but what impressed Tige was that the sifting had been just about completed in one day—very difficult and very unusual.

Claude worried off a cud of day's work, pocketed the plug and spat aside before saying, "Not too much feed down here, Tige."

The young man sat his saddle in solemn thought for a while. "Then we might have to trail down-country a mite early, because yesterday in town I looked up all the holdings adjoinin' us and there ain't anything up for sale or lease."

Claude's aquiline features were tough-set when

he said, "Ship early—take low dollar. Folks say that is an axiom, but it's sure true enough." He lifted a reinhand. "Care to ride down through? Might be something you'd want to cut back."

They both knew that was unlikely. When Claude made a cut Tige had yet to be dissatisfied about it. Tige shook his head. "No need." He waited briefly, then also said, "Old Edson Black had a stroke. He could die any day."

Remembering what his sister had said the previous day, he fidgeted slightly, then added more. "Or the old bastard might live five, six years. If he'd die I kind of got a feelin' Jess and Big Bill might want to leave the country. They might sell out."

Claude chewed, then said, "Good meadow over there. Good grassland the whole piece, except where it goes up into the timbered slopes. Sure would be handy. Adjoins Flesh-knife all along the east, and some of the southeast boundary line."

Claude spat, gazed mechanically out over the spread-out motley cut, spat and also said, "Suppose the old devil lives, five, six years?"

Tige had been unhappily considering this since last night. "Then he'd spoil things for us. We got to do something long before that anyway."

Freeman agreed. "I'd say we got to do something either this spring, this summer, or at the latest this autumn. Otherwise Flesh-knife ain't goin' into the winter with enough dry feed to

70

make it through." He tugged at his gloves. "Or—we got to go back and cull harder, make up a drive of mostly she-stock, which'll mean all the building up we been doin' the last few years will go down the road."

They turned back in the general direction of the home place, but angled westerly to look at whatever was still in the vicinity of the marking-ground, which was where they had made the cut.

Over there, the animals were superior just about any way a rider looked at them. Tige considered half a dozen heavy young cows and commented on the need to get them, all they could find like them, up north towards the foothills.

Claude nodded without comment. These things were the details every man on Flesh-knife understood. They did not require any palaver. Claude spat and rode slouched and thoughtful on the way back to the yard. He said very little until just before they were entering the yard out back by the working-corrals, then his comment could have been a loose generalization.

"Feller gets a choice now and then to get bigger or get littler, or just set still and mark time. The way costs been gettin' lately seems to me if a feller don't grow the times will gobble him up."

They off-saddled with the blood-red sun at their backs, with fleecy high clouds pink-tinted and frothy over in the east, and with Buttercup over on the porch of her cookshack leaning against a

71

porch-upright, fat arms crossed, like a mahogany carving.

There was no sign of Bertha, nor did her brother think of this.

The other riders had all come in and were over at the bunkhouse with their usual noise and laughter, flying insults and good-natured chousing.

Tige headed for the mainhouse, his rangeboss walked to the bunkhouse, and over on her porch Buttercup unlocked big arms and turned without even a grunt to go inside.

It would be a while before supper yet. Even as the days grew longer, daylight lingered well into evening, suppertime on Flesh-knife was the same, had always been the same under the heavy Sioux squaw, and would no doubt continue to be the same as long as she ruled at the cookshack.

She had cooked for Tige's father and his riding crews. To those who remembered her from back then, there was no sign of any change, not in her bearing, her grim outlook, nor in her unsmiling appearance.

But Buttercup had learned one thing and had learned it well; she knew how to cook for hungry rangemen; knew how to make the best strong black coffee, along with buckwheat cakes which would stick to a man's innards through the most grueling, long bruising days even at the marking-ground.

This evening she was more stonily impassive than usual as she worked, getting everything ready before she went out and beat the triangle, because once they came on the run there would be no second chance to make things ready.

She looked up when a man entered from out across the cookshack porch, something she discouraged unless they had been summoned. It was the one rider who had more right even than she had in the cookshack. He said, "Have you seen my sister, Buttercup?"

"Went riding," replied the dour older woman. "Goes riding almost every day."

"Well, but she usually gets back before this, Buttercup."

The squaw shrugged and went over to fill each fist with knives and forks. She returned to the long table without looking up or speaking.

Tige regarded her with the identical exasperation he had viewed her over the years since childhood—only then he had been afraid of her. "Did you see her ride out?"

"Yes."

"Did she happen to tell you where she'd be riding?"

"No."

"Well . . . which way did she ride?"

Buttercup straightened up and flung out a big arm to gesture eastward. "Over there." She let the arm drop to her side and stood looking steadily at Tige.

He had no difficulty with her implication. "The Black place, you mean?"

"Yes. I told her it's no good, stay away from over there. Maybe she didn't go over there this time, but other times she has. I tell you so you can make her stop it."

Tige scratched. "Well; the old man over there almost died with a stroke and she helped 'em a little."

"That old man is no good," exclaimed the Indian woman. "He killed."

"Gawddammit I'm getting sick and tired of havin' people tell me that—you included," Tige exploded at her. They stood rigidly regarding one another for a moment, then Buttercup leaned and went stonily back to setting her long supper table.

Tige felt bad. He liked her in spite of the things she had done to make this difficult. Right now he felt miserable enough to apologize but he knew Buttercup. The moment he opened his mouth to speak again, even to apologize, she would stamp over to the stove with her broad back to him, and she would remain in that posture until he departed.

He sighed and walked out upon the porch—and saw Bertha coming from the north in an easy lope. He stormed down off the porch.

She had no inkling a storm was approaching as she loped on in, swung off out front and led the horse inside to be off-saddled.

He hit the doorway with both spurred feet and

said, "Where the hell you been all day, Bertha?"

She turned very slowly and stared out at him. She knew his temperament, had known it since they had been children, and she had usually over the years excused many flashes of uncontrolled anger. But they were no longer children.

"What did you say, Tige?"

"You darned well heard what I said! Where in hell you been?"

She remained solidly in place holding both reins of her impatient horse. "It is none of your darned business where I've been," she hurled at him, anger making her green eyes sparkle even in the poor light.

He teetered upon the edge of an explosion. As they stood staring she spoke again, in the same low-toned, crisp tone of voice.

"Tige; it's been almost fifteen years since we've fought. . . . I haven't been where you think, I haven't been over to the Black ranch, nor even near it." She drew down a fresh breath. "Now— can we stop this?"

He lost much of the stiffness. Moments later he twisted self-consciously, embarrassed all the way through. It had not been *her,* it had been the other confounded female on Flesh-knife, which had annoyed him.

"Yeah, well," he told her, "I was wrong. Excuse me."

She turned without another word and proceeded

to swing off the saddle, then she removed the bridle and took the horse by a halter-shank out back. He followed as far as the rear barn opening and waited until she was returning to also say, "That was bad of me warn't it?"

She stopped close, looked up, and smiled. "Yes, it was bad. I wasn't expecting it. Tige; what's bothering you? Not culling close enough; the need for more land?"

"I expect that's it. Yeah, that's it." He followed her to the harness-pole where she had flung the saddle and stood aside while she draped the bridle. "You didn't see the Blacks?"

"No."

"I was wondering if maybe you had, and if you'd maybe asked around about them stayin' on after the old man dies."

She turned with a sigh. "Tige; you *know* me better than that. I wouldn't ask them something like that for any reason at all . . . Take the cattle to the uplands, why don't you?"

"May have to," he unhappily conceded.

She failed to see anything wrong with that. "You'll have to make a line-camp up there, won't you? And keep a man or two to watch the cattle and kill varmints, won't you?"

He said, "Yeah," beginning once again to resent her ability to touch the exact issue, and to resent her knowing enough to talk this way to him. "It'd be a lot better down here."

"But what's available?"

He looked out into the settling dusk without speaking.

She leaned upon the harness-pole watching his rather handsome, strong profile. "All right. Next time I ride over there I'll ask. But I can almost tell you in advance what there answer will be."

He smiled as he faced around. "Just ask, and if they get curious you can tell them there probably could be buyers found."

"Mention you and Flesh-knife?"

His smile became an instantaneous flash of irritability. "Of course not. They wouldn't sell to a Johnson. At least I wouldn't in their boots. Just tell them there's likely someone over in town who'd likely buy them out."

Her brows swung down slowly. "You're not doing this honestly," she told him. "This isn't like you, Tige."

"Just do it, Bertha. We got to have the land." He smiled into her tilted face, then turned abruptly and with long strides headed for the cookshack.

She went as far as the front opening and turned towards the mainhouse. She was hungry enough to chew the tail off a sidewinder, but she had not made a practice of eating when the men were. Not because she disliked their company but because her presence visibly inhibited them and if ever there was a time when range men deserved to be able to say exactly what they thought, and felt, it was after the day's work had been completed.

An hour later she went down there, through full darkness and after the on-going poker game was loudly under way in the lighted old bunkhouse.

Her brother must have decided to sit in for a few hands because he had not appeared at the mainhouse.

She walked in, caught the dark look from Buttercup, and ignored it to go amiably over and fill her own plate and draw off her own coffee.

Buttercup worked with her back to the rest of the room. Neither of them said a word as Bertha ate, drank coffee, and eventually arose to sink her plate, utensils and cup into the tub of greasy water near the stove where Buttercup was beginning the worst chore of them all, the wash-up.

"Your brother was looking for you," the Indian woman said, and did not look around at Bertha.

"He found me—at the barn, but thanks anyway. Something had him fired up."

"Hummpphh. . . ."

"Buttercup, what was Bart Flack like? I mean, of course I remember him, but as a child. What was he like?"

The Indian woman did not hesitate. She very seldom did, once she made up her mind to speak at all. "No good son of a bitch!"

Bertha rode out the surprise. "Really? In what way?"

Buttercup still did not raise her head. "Why do you ask me?"

"Curious is all, I guess. Tige and I were talking about him yesterday. But all I can remember was that my mother said once he was a good running-mate for my father."

"Around your father he was all right. Around everyone else, me too and I was a girl then, he was bad. Real bad."

"Mean?"

"Mean. Very mean man. Always looking for fight, always being mean."

Bertha leaned a moment wondering whether there was more to ask. She decided there was not. Buttercup had denounced the former rangeboss as blackly as she could; if she had to reply to additional questions she would repeat what she had already said.

Outside in the cooling night Bertha gazed thoughtfully over at the bunkhouse lights, then saw a lamp lighted in the parlor of the mainhouse and started to stroll slowly in that direction.

EIGHT
A Fresh Meeting

Two days later she rode the easterly range, starting early and reaching the far forested side-hills before the sun was even close to its meridian.

She felt mean and under-handed, riding in like this, pretending to be one thing, and being over there for something altogether different.

She was perfectly satisfied that both Jess and Big Bill knew who she was by now. The doctor had not told them, but surely their father had. He would have reason to, she told herself, swinging along the uphill trail to the spot where she had first encountered Bill Black, in the process of creating a cougar trap.

Not that it mattered, and in fact the situations which had evolved out of this, when she had been inadvertently prevented from explaining to them who she was, were funny—in one way—in another way those situations were a little spooky.

It appeared to her almost as though some force, or some kind of influencing power had stepped in at each crucial moment to prevent her from saying she was Weaver Johnson's daughter.

Then she came around the last spending slow curve of trail and saw smoke arising thinly, as though they'd built their breakfast fire early this morning.

There was no other sign of life though, as she threaded down out of the trees to the open country and boosted her mount over into a slow lope.

As before, when she tied up someone appeared in the doorway. This time it was the older brother rather than Jess.

He came to the edge of the porch and stood massively watching. When she finished loosening the cincha and making fast her tie-rope, and he still had said nothing she looked up at him a little skeptically and said, "Good morning, Mister Black."

He nodded. "Good morning."

She waited, but he added nothing to that, no name at all, so she approached the stairs as she said, "How is your father today?"

He gallantly stepped aside. "See for yourself, ma'am . . . I can tell you one thing; he's written on the slate three times now, asking if you'd be coming back."

She stopped close, looking upwards. "You could have sent me word."

"How; I don't even know your name?"

He pushed the door fully open for her to enter. From inside there was a nice smell of cooking meat, and when she stepped inside, the windows were still uncovered so that sunshine came in making the drab old parlor almost gay.

She turned. "Is your father resting?"

Big Bill crossed the room in giant strides and paused at the far closed doorway. "I expect he'll be resting all right. He don't do much else. But he'd be happy enough to rouse out of it for you."

Bill did not move clear of the doorway, though, and for a man of his size to be moved it would have taken a lot more strength than Bertha had; it might even have taken more power than a saddle-horse had.

She gazed calmly but enquiringly over at him.

"The name," he said.

"Bertha." She checked herself up short, unwilling to say the rest of it. Then she did it anyway. "Johnson. Bertha Johnson."

Big Bill did not blink an eye. He stepped to one side, leaned down to open the door and allowed her to pass into the stuffy little room without speaking to her again, until she went over and had to lean close to see his father in the old trundle-bed, because someone had put that blanket back across the rear-wall window again.

"We figured sunlight'd be bad for him."

She sighed, caught a flicker in the old man's unwatering eye, smiled, gently lay a hand upon his cheek, then went deliberately over and rolled back the blanket at least half-way. Immediately, there was golden light.

She returned to bedside, held up the slate and wrote clearly upon it, "Why didn't you tell your sons who I was?"

The old man's focusing eye read, flicked to her face, then returned to the slate. She leaned to help him sit a little, and put chalk in his usable hand.

"I didn't want them to run you away," he wrote to her, and let the chalk fall atop the blankets as he twisted his face.

The ravages were finally settling into lines and

creases on the afflicted side of his face. They had done that much, and more, to his nerves and muscles immediately after his affliction, but only now was the extent of his ailment becoming apparent in his features.

It was worse than that other instance of this same difficulty she had treated back in Nebraska.

She smiled and asked if they were feeding him well. He nodded clumsily. "And bathing you?" He raised his using hand to annoyedly dash water from the fixed, feelingless eye, then seemed almost to blush.

She turned. Bill had been watching, listening, and not moving nor making a sound. He hardly seemed to take his eyes off her, but the expression itself was unreadably blank.

"If he isn't washed every few days he'll get running sores," she told the large man. "You could dust his backsides with flour after you bathe him, and if gets bedsores, use goose grease . . . If you'll heat water and fetch in the tub I'll help you—show you how, this one time."

Bill glanced over her head at his father, then looked down into her lifted face—and reddened. "Jess and I could take care of that. He's out checkin' for drift right now, but directly he gets back we'll do it."

She liked Big Bill. He was—some way or other—honest and forthright. What made her half smile now was the discovery that he was also able to be embarrassed. She had to resist a temptation to tease him a little. Instead, she turned back when the old man thumped his bedside with his good fist.

She hoisted him, and this time Bill helped. They propped him with the slate in his lap. He wrote, "Let her show you, boy. I owe her. Whatever she wants, you listen to her."

Bill read, and scowled at his father. The old man's one good eye looked steadily back until Bill shrugged and said, "Paw, in a little while." He then took Bertha by the arm and left the bedroom with her, eased the door closed and pointed to a chair where he wanted her to sit.

She went over there but she did not sit in the chair.

"Are you Tige Johnson's sister?" he asked.

She nodded, and waited.

He studied her. "I remember—you got married and moved out of the territory, over to Ohio or somewhere."

"Nebraska, not Ohio. Is that why you had to close the door, Mister Black?"

"No. I had to know what Johnson you were. Does my Paw know you are Weaver's girl?"

"Yes. I told him several days ago. I was surprised this morning that he had not told you boys. Then he explained about that." She felt like sitting but did not do it. "Do you want to throw me out?"

Big Bill looked mildly irritated by that. He refused to honor it by answering, he instead said, "Miss Johnson. . . ."

She was not Miss Johnson and had not been in more than seven years, but here in the land where she had been born and had grown up, and where her family was sufficiently prominent for the name to have impact, she would always be a Johnson.

"Miss Johnson . . . I don't figure to sound ungrateful . . ."

"Then don't," she cut in to exclaim. "I'm doing what I'd do for anyone . . . even the man sent to prison for killing my father. Does that answer anything you have in mind?"

"*My* mind, maybe," he conceded soberly.

"Your brother. . . . ?"

"He's different, Miss Johnson."

"The other day when I was here . . . but he didn't know who I was, did he? I forgot that." She looked around at the chair and finally sat down. "What do you suggest, Mister Black—that I never come back?"

"Well . . . Does your brother know you came over here?"

"He knows," she replied, and for the first time her eyes wavered and left his face. "And if you want to know whether he approves—no, Mister Black he doesn't approve. So—neither your brother nor my brother approves. Does that mean

85

anything to your father or me? I think not a darned thing. What does it mean to you, Mister Black?"

He clearly was unaccustomed to this kind of blunt and outspoken female, but his reaction to her candor was different from the reaction of her brother, whom she antagonized by being frank. Big Bill looked very faintly amused. He did not interrupt, and while she spoke he did not take his eyes off her.

Then he said, "I don't disapprove, ma'am." He shifted stance. "In fact I figure you've done more for Paw than that pill-roller from Frontera. For a fact Paw sets considerable store by you."

She began to lose a little of her defiant stiffness. She even loosened her jacket, which she had not removed as yet. He kept watching her, then said, "Coffee?" and moved towards the stove.

She knew how men like this made their coffee. She was not an enthusiastic coffee-drinker at any time but here and now . . . "No thank you. Did the doctor tell you what to feed your father—what food he shouldn't have?"

Bill nodded from over where he was drawing off a cup of coffee. "Yes'm." He looked at her. "Sure you won't have a cup; we threw in two fist-fuls of fresh grounds this morning."

She sighed. "No thank you. Shall we bath him now?"

He did not leave the vicinity of the stove as he

sampled the coffee, still eyeing her across the cup-brim. "Directly," he conceded.

She wanted to smile. Instead she finally removed the riding jacket, turning slightly away as she did so. Even so, his eyes never left her.

From what appeared to be a very great distance there was a faint ripple of sound which she detected without being able to identify, and when she turned back Big Bill Black was trickling more hot java into his cup. He evidently had heard nothing.

She went over and peeked into the stewpot atop the stove where that simmering knot-fire was burning which was making smoke up the chimney. Bill said, "Rabbit."

She was surprised. It looked good and smelled delicious. "You prepared it?"

He finally did smile. "You sounded surprised. After enough years of tryin' I guess anyone can learn to be a tolerable cook."

She could have disputed that. From experience she had known a number of men who could scarcely boil water without burning it. But she did not wander from the topic as she replaced the stew-pot lid. "I'm sure you are talented, Mister Black," she told him and moved away as he said, "I'm a peaceable man, ma'm," and if he had said that as some kind of innuendo about the gundown many years ago, she had an answer.

"I am also peaceable, Mister Black."

"You don't hate the old man?"

She glanced sadly in the direction of the closed door. "How? Do you know how much time he has? Neither do I, Mister Black, but it could be a blessing if he could go soon. He is widely paralyzed, unable to help himself. He will not get better even though it may seem that he will for a while." She whirled. "Could you hate a man under those circumstances?"

He answered without any hesitation. "No, ma'm."

That distant, faint reverberation came riding down the airless day again, little more than a disturbed strata of still air. It seemed even more distant this time than when she had heard it earlier.

She thought it probably was very distant thunder. It would have to be very distant indeed, because there was not a cloud outside in the vault of high blue heaven.

Nevertheless she stepped to the window to throw a searching look up and around. From behind her Bill said, "Did you hear anything?"

With her back to him she said, "Far-away thunder, wasn't it?"

He answered slowly, indecisively. "Oh. Well maybe that's what it was. My first reaction was—gunfire."

She did not even consider such a thing, but her scanning of the far skies showed no clouds, not even over the distant mountains.

Bill put aside his empty cup and stirred the rabbit stew, replaced the lid and this time when the sounds arrived, they were borne upon a vagrant little ground-well breeze which came from the north.

It *was* gunfire. She listened, could scarcely believe what her mind told her, and slowly turned. Bill was at the stove, big wooden ladle poised in mid-air as he began to slowly stiffen while he made up his mind.

Then he put down the ladle with great deliberation, turned and crossed the room grabbing a booted carbine from beside the door on his way. He looked soberly at her and gave an order.

"You stay here with Paw."

NINE
Shockwaves!

She obeyed from habit, but not for long. When she saw him ride out of the barn-area astride the big chestnut gelding, she had just returned from peeking in upon his father. The stricken man was sleeping.

She moved on impulse to pick up her jacket and start toward the door. Her horse was dozing, perfectly satisfied to remain indefinitely where he had been standing. Nor did he act pleased when she yanked up the cincha, flung the reins and climbed aboard. He turned stiffly, his back humped beneath the saddle. She made no effort to spur him, which would certainly have precipitated the very battle the horse was considering. She let him walk for several hundred yards, until the bow left his back, his head came up a little, and he settled into an habitual gait. Then, finally, she set him towards the sidehill trail Bill Black had taken, and eased him over into a lope.

She did not catch sight of the big man up ahead somewhere, but she knew from the fresh dust in the air that he was not very far onward as she came around the sunshiny slope and burst across a clearing where the dust was even visible, with sunshine in the glade.

Those sounds, gunfire or whatever they had been, were no longer audible, but then they had not been consistently audible before. Nor was she entirely satisfied in her mind that those had been gunshots.

She could not on the spur of the moment find an alternative which had the same sound, but she could not imagine why there would be gunfire up here, unless there happened to be some hunters—perhaps townsmen from Frontera—down there, and if that were so, why would they have fired so much?

She did not find any answers. She did not in fact look very hard for them as she followed this trail which she had not been over since childhood, if then, except for the brief period when she had ridden southward, into the Black yard, upon it.

Finally, where the trail climbed steadily, she had to haul the horse down to a slogging walk in order not to completely wind it, and up ahead she saw Big Bill doing the same thing astride his big chestnut gelding.

He was not aware of her closeness. He was sitting up there near the top-out of the slope, peering intently at something down the far side. She wanted to greet him, but while she was debating this with herself, he grunted and pointed his horse down the far slope.

She reached his vantage point and stopped dead in her tracks.

It seemed to be a considerable distance northward, but there was no mistaking the big herd of cattle. They were Flesh-knife animals. They *had* to be; there was no other big band of livestock for many miles in all directions because except for the parcel where Bertha was sitting, and a little more of the same, all the land hereabouts belonged to Flesh-knife.

She sat frowning until something hit her in the pit of the stomach. Tige and Claude would not have deliberately done this. She remembered with vivid starkness all her brother had said about gaining control of the Black's range.

But it would not be like her brother to make a gather then deliberately drive it over onto the land of the Blacks.

Yet—how else explain what she saw down there, several hundred cattle spreading out now, but clearly having been driven over here. That many cattle would never come like this without being driven.

She started down the same slope Bill had taken earlier. Within moments she was down into an abysmal world of shadows and shade weaving back and forth upon what was a game trail but a well travelled one. Ahead, in certain places she had no difficulty at all detecting the fresh shod-horse marks dead ahead.

There was not a sound anywhere. No gunfire, no bawling cattle out there, but most significant to her as she fought back an urge to hasten along, there were no birds in the surrounding forest.

Premonitions arose from many causes, but with Bertha the fear became solid and unchanging when she began to believe that in fact that most certainly *had been* gunfire.

She was scarcely aware of her own movement while the horse made his way down-slope, then tipped back when he reached level country and widened his stride a little because he thought the person on his back was going to ask him to do this anyway.

She saw one riderless horse cropping grass, reins dragging, saddle snug on its back. That was all she saw until she got a further half-mile along, then she saw Bill Black standing with his animal in dappled tree-fringe shade near where the grass-land began. He was gazing out at all those grass-cropping cattle.

He turned, hearing her, and waited until she was well in sight before making the certain identification, and turning back to the sights before him.

When she got down close and stepped off to loop reins and walk ahead, he looked around one more time, then, as though becoming fully aware of her for the first time, he turned.

She came over and considered the nearest cattle. The Flesh-mark brand was easily discernible. She saw that riderless horse again and started down there without saying a word.

For a while they were not in communication. Not until he trailed along, recognized the horse even before he was close enough to read the mark, and said, "That's Jess's sorrel."

She saw the shoulder-brand and halted, baffled by all of it. "Those are Flesh-knife cattle."

He ignored that to say, "The shooting . . . where is my brother? Where are the men who drove those cattle over onto our range?"

He stepped away from her, twisting to glance along the lower, treeless fringe of slope where visibility was excellent. He suddenly started walking.

She turned back to what was visible, trying to make some kind of sense out of all this. There should have been at least two or three Flesh-knife rangeriders in sight. It made little sense to drive a herd this size over here, then just abandon it where it would certainly cross over into Black cow range. . . . Unless that had been the idea.

Bill called to her. She turned and went towards the sound of his voice, following along the lower fringe of trees.

He was standing loosely, leaning slightly against an old pine with no limbs for almost a hundred feet straight up. She stepped beside him and caught her breath.

The man lying there on his side as though he were napping was one of her brother's riders; a young cowboy named Clint Anderson. She did not wait for Bill to do it, but went ahead, leaned and eased the dead man over. He had two bullet wounds, one high through the chest, near the center, one lower through his thickest part.

There was no gun in his hip-holster but his riding gloves had been neatly tucked under the shellbelt and were still there.

She twisted, saying the dead man's name. Big Bill acted as though he had not heard her. He stared a long while at dead Clinton Anderson then pushed up off the tree and began a very slow, very dragging search of the roundabout area through tall grass and over the lower reaches of sidehill forest.

Bertha found Anderson's six-gun in the grass as she was going back towards the riderless horse. It had been fired three times. She carried it with her as she joined Bill in his search, and when he saw it she passed it over.

There had been a fight, no question about that, and evidently her brother and his rangeboss had left in a run afterwards. Just as clearly, Jess Black had not left, unless he had done it on foot which was very unlikely when there was nothing wrong with his saddle-horse.

Bertha was dreading the discovery for a long while before she made it.

Jess was lying in a half-curl where he had struck a tree and had bounded forward as he was falling. The bullet had pierced his head from front to back. He probably had no more than one second to react before death overtook him.

She turned her back, went to a punky deadfall and leaned there without calling for Bill. When he missed her and came looking, he stopped stone-still without seeming to even breathe for a full five minutes.

Bertha went back to the riderless horse and led it through the trees, tied it near Bill and turned without a word to go back up the trail where she had left her own horse.

It was a long ride back to Flesh-knife even when someone rode swiftly. She was too sick at heart to want to get back. Any way she viewed it those Flesh-knife cattle had no business on Black range. Her brother and Claude had been talking about Black range. Her brother had even mentioned its desirability to her.

The conclusions were inescapable. When she had the yard in sight there was not a soul down there. Even the corrals out behind the barn were empty.

She turned off deliberately to verify this before entering the yard from the west, and Buttercup, over on her cookshack porch, saw her enter the yard. She waved, something she never did, but Bertha did not wave back. She rode on in, swung off at the barn and led the horse inside to be off-saddled.

There was not a sound anywhere around, so after caring for the animal she crossed to the cookshack. Buttercup brought her coffee at the long table without a word.

Bertha ignored it. "Where are the men?" she asked, and Buttercup shrugged. She had not seen them.

"Did they all ride out together this morning?" Bertha asked.

Buttercup thought, then shook her head and made one of her sweeping arm gestures. "Three go that way, south, your brother and one other man go west, the way you come from just now."

Bertha studied Buttercup's smooth, coarse brown face. If three men went south . . . "Was Clinton Anderson one of the men who rode south?"

"Yes."

Bertha turned, saw the cup and lifted it finally, with something close to a feeling of relief. Her brother may not have been over there after all.

Buttercup waited in speculative silence for a long while, studying Bertha's face, then she turned back to her stove and became busy over there until someone rode into the yard, a sound she detected despite the popping of the stove's wood-box. Bertha did not hear a thing; had no idea anyone had arrived until she saw Buttercup head for the door and peer out.

Bertha left the coffee cup and strode forth. The rider was her brother, and he was sitting his saddle down in front of the barn looking either baffled or angry, in an event his face was creased into a deep frown.

She walked out there. He saw her, scarcely spared her a glance, then swung to the ground and started into the barn.

She halted him in the doorless wide opening with a question. "Where is your foreman, Tige? Where are the men who rode with him? And where did he pick up the cattle he drove over to the Black place?"

Tige looked at her, his baffled look becoming deeper. ". . . The Black place? I just come from south where he had that bunch of sifted stuff, old gummer cows and the like."

"Were they down there?"

97

"No. That's what I came back up here looking for Claude about."

She moved to the tie-rack and leaned upon it looking him squarely in the face. "Clinton Anderson is dead and Jess Black is dead, and your sifted cattle are over on the Blacks' grassland at the base of the easterly hills."

He was stunned.

She let him digest that then she also said, "Claude wouldn't do something like that on his own, would he Tige?"

He did not answer. He turned and reached furiously to pull up the loosened cinch on his horse. She watched, then stepped around the tie-rack to get closer as she said, "Don't go over there."

He flashed an antagonistic look at her and increased his motions. She grabbed the reins and held them. "Tige, I left Bill Black over there more than an hour ago with his dead brother. Don't even go near the Black place today."

He was ready to mount, had his left hand on the horn without the reins and started to lean to snatch them from her, but she stepped farther back, holding the reins in fierce grip.

"Whatever happened, if you ride over there now, Tige, you're going to start it up all over again . . . Did you send Claude and those cattle over there?"

"Send them? What kind of a damnfool thing is that to ask? Of course I didn't send them. Now give me those reins!"

"Are you going over there?"

"You're damned right I am!"

She stepped close, released the throat-latch, yanked off the bridle, and the astonished horse looked left and right because he had never before been unbridled before having his saddle removed first. Then he jumped away and trotted aimlessly out across the yard where Buttercup saw him like that and clucked to herself several times before going back inside the cookshack.

Tige was white in the face. His sister did not yield one step. "Wait. Let it stand the way it is for a day, Tige. Bill will shoot you on sight."

"I didn't have a damned thing to do with—"

"Then let it wait; don't go over there. Please, Tige . . . I saw Clinton Anderson dead with two bullet holes in him, and the younger Black with a wound through his skull from front to back." She stepped around him and went to the harness-pole to drape his bridle. They both ignored the bewildered horse in the middle of the yard.

"Why did they do it?" he asked her. "Claude never did anything like that before. Bertha, it don't make a lick of sense . . . Why?"

She could have mentioned his own continuing comments about the need for Black range. Instead she said, "Where is the man who rode out with you today? Buttercup said you and a rider went west."

Her brother answered indifferently, as though

this detail had no importance. "That was Jett. I left him down on the lower range making a track. We never figured they'd been drove, Sis, we figured they had started to drift over in that direction . . . Never would have figured anything—like this. My gawd!"

TEN
In the Wake of Gunfire

Blake Hobart listened stonily to the pair of men facing him across his jailhouse desk in Frontera, his latent sense of foreboding coming increasingly to dominate him, and when Claude Freeman stopped talking Sheriff Hobart said, "I knew it would happen. Gawddammit I knew it!" He looked almost pitiably at the pair of rumpled rangemen. "What was he doing out there?"

Claude said, "Waiting, I figure. He'd seen us movin' the herd and was hid up along the first fringe of trees on horseback, like I been tellin' you, and when we commenced to swing the herd so's it wouldn't get onto his range, he took a shot and hit Clint Anderson, who was over on that side of the herd. Hit Clinton through the body. Clinton fired back. Then—hell—like I told you, young Black come out of the trees like a crazy man shootin' at the cattle, at us, and he killed Anderson that time. Then me and Ike here fought back. Black went down—and we run for it

100

because we didn't want to have to shoot the other one and we figured he might hear the noise and show up."

"You're plumb sure you killed Jess?"

"Pretty sure, Sheriff, but we didn't hang around to go look at him. I'll tell you one thing, he was hit in the head and I ain't heard of too many folks walking away from that kind of wound."

"Did you go back and look at Anderson?"

"Didn't have to," replied the sweaty and disheveled rangeboss. "I saw him get hit that second time. He was dead before he hit the ground."

Sheriff Hobart pondered. The question now was to locate Big Bill Black. If he was perhaps on his way to town right now. . . .

"You boys stay right here in the jailhouse."

Claude looked displeased. "We got to get back. For all we know that crazy big one'll skulk over like their paw done, and ambush Tige or Jett, the rider with Tige. You know that's a bushwhacking clan, Sheriff."

"If you believe that," responded Hobart, "then you'll know why I want you boys to remain right here."

"Where you going?" the rangeboss asked.

"To make a little posse," replied Sheriff Hobart, arising with slow displeasure. "When you fellers head back you'll ride with us. I'm not going to have any more of this if I can help it." He considered Claude and the rider called Ike. "I want your word you'll be here when I get back."

They agreed, and Blake Hobart headed out. He went first to the gunsmith's shop. Not only the gunsmith, but some of the cowboys and freighters who hung around down there, were a good source for possemen. He also visited the saloon, but because it was suppertime there were only a few unmarried, older men at the bar, none of them suitable in Blake Hobart's view, as possemen.

He eventually recruited two men from the livery-barn, the gunsmith, and a man named Beeman who was out front of the stage company's corralyard eating an apple. Beeman was a small rancher in the easterly hills. He was glad of an opportunity to make some extra money.

Hobart's posse, counting himself, numbered four riders. They all had booted carbines and jackets when they stood out front of the jailhouse silently watching Claude and Ike climb aboard their ridden-hard horses to start back.

Along the roadway men were beginning to guess something was seriously wrong; they congregated here and there, beckoned to other men, and watched as Sheriff Hobart, his three possemen, and those two Flesh-knife riders walked their horses southward down out of town.

Frontera had been speculating for years on the eventual face-down everyone figured had to occur between Tige Johnson and the Blacks. That it had not ever happened did not alter confirmed opinions one whit. It *would* happen, they sagely said, someday.

But no one knew what had occasioned Sheriff Hobart's departure southward with possemen because as yet no one in Frontera had heard talk of what had occurred on the range.

They speculated though, and as was often the case, they eventually through a process of elimination, whittled it down to exactly what had happened.

All Blake Hobart thought of as he rode along, was prevention. He was not even distraught over two men having been killed. He did not know Clint Anderson and he did not deep-down, feel that Jess was a real loss. He had had trouble with the fierce younger son of Edson Black over the years. He had never liked Jess, and now what he really felt was relief. With Jess out of it, there might still exist a way to stop a bloody range war or another gundown.

Claude was behind him, riding with the uncommunicative Flesh-knifer called Ike. Claude was detailing the story again for the silent and fascinated possemen. Nor did Clause make any aspect of the occurrence favorable to Jess Black. He steadfastly accused Jess of deliberately trying to bushwhack all the Flesh-knife riders, and told how he did in fact ambush one, Clinton Anderson.

Blake would have liked to have told Claude to shut up. But by the time this idea arrived, Claude had indoctrinated the possemen into the conviction that one of the Blacks—whose father had been imprisoned for bushwhacking—had deliberately ambushed and killed one Flesh-knife rider and attempting to kill others all the while that those Flesh-knife riders were minding their own business, were on their own land, and had no idea they were riding into someone's gun-sights.

Eventually, though, down where they left the roadway heading in the direction of the Flesh-knife yard, Blake said, "Ride up here with me," to the range-boss, and when they were riding stirrup, he then said, "Tell me again—why was you fellers up there, that close to the boundary line, with those cattle?"

Freeman's reply was perfect. "For the feed, Sheriff. That was our cull-bunch; lot of old gummer cows in there that can't crop close to the ground. We took them over to the northeastern range because the feed was tall and good over there. We got to keep those critters fat because they shrink like hell anyway once we commence driving them down to rail's-end. You see?"

Blake 'saw'. He had been a rangeman once himself, and he had spent his entire life in range country. Everything Claude had said rang with truth and conviction. In fact, it *was* the truth, every word of it.

Sheriff Hobart asked where Tige Johnson had been throughout the fight. Again, Claude told the absolute truth. The last he had seen of his employer had been shortly after breakfast when they had all been at the barn saddling up.

"You could have rode to the home-place instead of streaking it for town," muttered Hobart, and again Claude had the perfect answer.

"I figured going to Tige would only make him head over to settle with Bill Black. I figured you would want to nip things in the bud."

That was true, but Sheriff Hobart rolled his lines, fished forth his makings and lowered his head in grave thought as he rode along manufacturing a cigarette. When he lit up he looked at the late-day sky, decided since it was early summertime, daylight would linger for some time yet, then he blew smoke and turned to regard Ike. The rangerider with Claude Freeman had not opened his mouth five times since arriving in town. Some men were affected like that by death, especially violent death.

They made a diversion to the easterly range because Sheriff Hobart wanted to see the cattle— and those two dead men.

They found the cattle without any trouble, scattered out still cropping tall grass, but they did not find either the loose saddle-horse, nor the pair of corpses. They saw blood, though, and that was convincing enough, so they turned back in the direction of the home-place on Flesh-knife range and by the time they reached the yard there was a thin, long stain of near-twilight up across the rearward heavens.

Bertha saw them coming from a mile out and went to find her brother. They then stood in the barn-opening watching, neither of them speaking when they recognized the lawman and his posse-riders.

Tige turned, just once, as though to irritably comment about his sister remaining out there when men were talking, but something in her expression, and down along the square curve of her jaw, held him silent.

Blake Hobart hauled up, nodded, and without any preliminaries said, "You know what hap-pened, do you, Tige? Jess Black got shot and so did one of your men. Claude and this other feller run to town to fetch me back." Without adding more, nor waiting to be invited to dismount, Sheriff Hobart swung off, stepped to the tie-rack and looped his reins without thinking about it.

Tige scowled at his rangeboss. "What the hell caused it, Claude?"

"Well, I decided they had to be moved off the south range. You saw how they was droppin' off day by day, so I and Ike here and Clint turned them northeast where they'd get enough decent feed for them to hold their own until the time to trail them south . . . We'd scarcely got up there

106

than this crazy son of a bitch in the trees shot Clint, then tried to bushwhack us too. We fought him off, shot him down, then figured we'd better get the law or the other one'd be out there skulkin' around tonight to kill the rest of us. They always been a bunch of murderers."

It sounded as plausible now as it had sounded up in Frontera. Bertha had a feeling, so she groped for some flaw and finally came up with one, which actually, on Flesh-knife, was not a flaw at all. Still, she said, "Claude, did Tige tell you to move that cull herd?"

The long-faced rangeboss—who had never liked Bertha, nor having her on the ranch—looked steadily at her for a moment without opening his mouth. Then her brother answered irritably.

"Bertha, Claude moves cattle all the time on his own. Always has. That's how we run the ranch, damn it."

Sheriff Hobart listened, killed his smoke under foot and said, "Folks, I got to go over to the Black place." He looked around at the lighted cook-shack. "Go have supper or something, only stay here, don't leave the yard until I get back." He turned to his possemen. "Keep 'em here, gents, for their own darned safety."

As Hobart turned to step back across leather Tige's sister moved over to say, "I'll ride with you, Sheriff. In case old Mister Black has had a relapse after the death of his son."

107

Blake faintly frowned at her. "How do you know his son is dead?"

"Because I was with Bill Black when we found him. He had been shot through the head. He was dead. So was my brother's cowboy—the one they called Clint." She waited, then turned to get a horse and as Blake Hobart watched her go, one of the possemen wagged his head.

"I wouldn't take no woman where there's likely to be bad trouble, Blake."

Tige offered the rebuttal to that. "She's been caring for old Ed Black since his stroke. Been a sort of nurse over there. She'll be safe." Tige thought, then changed that to: "She'll be as safe over there as anyone—today."

But Sheriff Hobart did not cherish the idea of riding into the Black yard—with a woman companion. Bad enough to go over there alone, or even with his possemen, right at this juncture, but with a woman. . . .

She came forth leading a rigged-out leggy black horse. She had an old jacket on which she had found hanging on a peg in the barn. She looked sturdy enough to be as strong as a man when she came up under their collective stares, and said, "Sheriff, should we take a lantern, just in case . . . ?"

He snorted, disdaining to even answer, and swung up across his horse's back, looking less and less enthralled at the prospect ahead. On the other hand, she just might be the one guarantee he could have, arriving over there in the dusk at a time when Big Bill Black would certainly not be so grief-stricken he would not grab a gun at the first sound of a shod horse coming out of the gloom into his yard.

The Flesh-knife men had been talking among themselves. Jett and Tige had been completely in the dark. Claude, with his story intact after having been repeated so often, was down to answering questions, and the possemen, on the ground now that it was clear they were not to ride any farther, were loosening girths and getting ready to look after their animals.

No one heeded the sturdy, dark silhouette over on the cookshack porch, arm poised to rattle the triangle for supper. No one as yet had thought to tell Buttercup there would be one less Flesh-knifer to feed this evening.

Tige seemed to have something on the tip of his tongue when his sister swung up and briefly sat beside Sheriff Hobart before they both turned to leave the yard. Whatever it was, Tige did not say it, and a mile out, when the riders were angling slightly more to the east than the north, Sheriff Hobart had a question for Bertha.

"What did you mean back there when you asked if Claude had Tige's permission to move those cattle?"

"Just exactly what I said, Sheriff."

Hobart sighed and tried to rephrase it. "Does Claude move cattle without askin' Tige?"

"Usually he does, yes, but what was bothering me. . . ." She thought it over before going any further, then decided to say it anyway. "What bothered me, Sheiff, is that Flesh-knife is getting low on feed and there has been talk lately of where to get more."

He turned, staring at her. "The Black range . . . ?"

"Tige mentioned it, yes, but not in this way, not as though he ever even thought about just driving roughshod over the Blacks." She rode a few yards before also saying, "But this was not something Tige had a hand in. He was as astonished as he could be when I returned from the Black range today and told him what had happened—how I figured it had happened—our cattle being driven onto the Black range, and Jess Black exploding the way he must have done when he started shooting at them." She met Blake Hobart's level look.

"Sheriff; Claude Freeman had the authority to organize that kind of a drive. Obviously he did it; led Clinton and Ike over here. That much is clear as daylight, isn't it?"

He nodded. "Seems so."

"I know my brother very well, Sheriff. He was dumbfounded when I told him of that drive—of his cattle being pushed over onto Black rangeland. He did not know a thing about it."

110

Sheriff Hobart was less than convinced. "Your brother isn't my kinsman like he is to you, so I'll just sort of hold off on my judgment for a while." He stood in his stirrups. "Can't see the house yet, can you?"

She did not have to stand in her stirrups; daylight was fast fading and the distance was still too great. She shook her head without speaking. In a way, she dreaded this ride. More to the point, she dreaded her destination.

ELEVEN
A Night's Beginning

With a man like Jess Black it was never difficult to guess a reaction, but Big Bill was different, not just in age and coloring, but also in his quietness under strain.

When Sheriff Hobart was tying up out front of the log barn across from the house, he shook his head dolorously to himself. Every ingredient for bad trouble was right here, this evening. The key would be Bill Black. As he turned to see if Bertha had tied up, he saw her gazing across the saddle-seat to the barn opening across from them.

Bill Black was standing there with a carbine fisted and his legs sprung wide, as though he had been expecting enemies, and was not yet convinced he was not looking at enemies.

Hobart said, "Good evening, Bill. I got down

111

here as fast as I could." He started around the tie-rack, then stopped as that one-handed Winchester shifted slightly, seemed to be rising. Bill ignored Blake Hobart and did not take his eyes off Bertha right up until he softly said, "Where is your brother tonight?"

She finished loosening the cincha, lowered her head, and replied gently. "Over at the home-place. Please just listen for a moment."

Bill used the carbine as a pointer and gestured for them to come over where he was. Inside the barn where a wavery little coal-oil lamp was burning, they saw the pair of dead men lying out full length upon the same soiled old square of wagon-top canvas.

Sheriff Hobart started over, halted where he could see the bullet holes, then let his shoulders droop as he silently remained looking down. Both dead men had died from bullets through the brain.

Hobart turned his head. "Did you see any of it, Bill?"

Black stepped closer, fell into the unsteady perimeter of lamplight and said, "No. I was at the house with her and when we heard it, I ran for a horse. But it'd been goin' on for some time by then, and when I got up there—this was all that was left, Jess dead, this Flesh-knife rider dead, and their cattle half on our range, half on their range . . . You know what they were trying to do, Blake? Drive their cattle onto our grass!"

Bertha could see the big knuckles gripping that Winchester tighten in a writhing way. The gun looked almost toy-like in that big, powerful fist.

Sheriff Hobart eyed Big Bill, a head full of thoughts he had no place for.

It was Bertha who spoke next when she asked Bill if he had told his father.

Bill scarcely more than flicked a glance in her direction when he said, "No. I haven't been to the house since I got back."

She frowned. "He's been alone in there all that time?"

That made Bill face her. His eyes were very dark, much darker than their customary gun-metal shade of grey, and his features were not particularly hard-set; they looked almost gentle in their relaxed manner. But not even a child would have mistaken the mood behind that almost-gentle expression.

She turned to leave the barn. He halted her when she was in the doorway when he said, "Don't tell him."

She nodded, then he tried to stumble through an explanation. "I—it'll have to do done, maybe in the morning . . . I'm afraid of what it will do to him. My brother was his favorite. He looked most like his wife." Bill paused, looking across where she gently nodded her head.

"I'll say nothing, but he needs looking after."

Bill nodded as she turned to cross through the dusk-mantled yard. Behind her, Sheriff Hobart said, "Tige didn't know anything about it until she got back from over here and told him."

Bill's voice rang with scorn when he said, "Do you believe that?"

Sheriff Hobart flushed. "That's what I think right this minute, and I got fair reason to believe it." He looked down again, wondering how to say he had always known Jess was fiery tempered. In the end he said nothing, but stood hip-shot gazing at the dead men until Big Bill went over to turn up the lampwick a little. It made the little lamp smoke but neither of them heeded that.

Bill said, "Blake, there is only one way that happened. They tried to push cattle over onto us up north of here where they didn't expect me or my brother to be. If it hadn't been like that, why didn't they push the cattle over onto our feed down south, closer to the mainhouse—because they knew darned well we'd catch them at it. Up there—where they didn't expect to get caught—they got caught anyway, and they fought, then broke and run for it."

"Run to town and my office," stated the lawman, turning finally so he would no longer be able to see the dead men. "Claude said Jess opened up on them while they were still on their side of the boundary line, Bill."

Black's retort was bitter. "What would you expect him to say? And don't tell me he did all that on his own."

"They told me about an hour back that this is exactly how it happened. I just told you—I don't believe, at this time, Tige had any idea Claude was going to push those cattle up here, and Bill— if they was on their own side of the line and Jess shot that cowboy. . . ."

"In the morning I'll take you up and show you tracks *on our side* for five hundred yards before they got their herd as far north as they were when Jess fought them. Blake, they were already tres- passin' all over us before Jess saw them. I can show you the sign of it."

Sheriff Hobart was willing to listen to it all, from both sides. That was his purpose in being out here. It was also his job. He did not even con- sider the possibility that he would not ultimately know the truth. What he worried about was the Winchester in the hand of the large man in the barn with him, and that gentle-seeming strange expression on the big man's face.

He took a chance and said, "Bill, I need your word that you won't go over there, won't leave your yard here for a few days."

"And then, Sheriff?"

"I left three possemen over there to make plumb certain they stay at home too . . . Well?"

"No," drawled the big man, gazing at his dead

brother in the wavery, yellow lampglow. "No promises of any kind, Sheriff."

Hobart's course was clear. He had the authority to back it up too, but he did not want to risk a fight and he knew the large man nearby, aside from still holding that Winchester, was in a dangerous frame of mind.

He rolled a cigarette, leaned to light it from the smoking lamp-chimney and straightened back without looking down. "I need some time to unravel it, Bill, and another killing won't help anyone." He made his plea in a quiet tone of voice without sounding either pleading or threatening. He had been in this predicament before, also, he was a good judge of men. He was willing to gamble that quiet reason would reach Big Bill Black, exactly as under reversed conditions it never would have reached Jess Black.

They were a long moment in silence. The only sounds were being made by tethered horses out front shifting weight now and then as they dozed.

Blake groped for another rational remark, and with a stroke of genius said, "Bill, the woman's been good for your old man. You maybe don't feel that you owe her, and I'm sure she'd never even think of it like that—but you *do* owe her. . . . Tige is her brother . . . Give me until tomorrow night. Stay on the place, right here close by the house, until I return tomorrow night." Blake started walking in the direction of the door, stopped and turned for his answer.

He did not get it.

From across the yard Bertha called in a fluting, high voice, and both men responded, Sheriff Hobart the first one out into the night but with Bill close at his heels. There had been an urgency in her voice neither had ever heard before, nor would they have had to hear it before to realize the sense of urgency behind it.

She was standing with the door closed at her back when they reached her, looking pale in the diluted star-shine. Bill's premonition pushed him ahead to say, "Paw . . . ?"

She nodded and led the way. Sheriff Hobart, hat in hand, lingered in the parlor while she went with Bill into the back bedroom.

She had lighted a lamp but the room was still corner-dark and dingy. The lamp-chimney contributed, it had not been cleaned in a long while.

The old man looked pale enough for his skin to be transparent. He was breathing hard and his eyes flickered. Bill leaned, murmured, and when there was no response he turned. She shook her head to indicate she knew no more than he knew.

She moved ahead, beside Bill, and leaned to lightly place a hand upon the motionless, useless hand of Edson Black. There was no response, nor could there have been, but when she removed the hand he seemed to feebly seek the touch. She reached for his other hand, closed her fingers down, and he responded. She smiled and motioned for Bill to bring a chair.

She sat with the old man, her warm fingers clinging to his colder ones, until his son tiptoed from the room, then she leaned to make certain coverlets were under his chin and that he was comfortable.

Bill saw Sheriff Hobart staring when he closed the door leaving her in there. He had nothing to say for a long while, but he went to the stove and filled two cups with coffee and handed one to Hobart.

The sheriff said, "He's alive? Is it another stroke?"

Bill did not know and shrugged, so Hobart offered to ride to town for the doctor. Bill neither accepted the offer nor rejected it, he stood gazing at the floor for a long while, drinking coffee and staring.

Bertha came out to them nearly an hour later, while Blake Hobart was trying to figure out a way to discuss the things which were vital to him, with these two people who were so intensely involved in the same things, but which seemed now not to hold their concern.

She said she did not think it was another stroke, but she had no idea what it was. Physically, he had not seemed much different than before; if

118

there were additional deterioration she had been unable to locate it.

He was conscious but would not write on the slate. He held her hand and seemed to soundlessly cry with his one good eye, the one functioning side of his face, but except for the way he clung to her he did not want to acknowledge that she was even there.

Sheriff Hobart looked with exasperation in the direction of the bedroom door. He was stymied. But he could not stand here all night, so he turned and said, "Bill, I've got to have your word— about what we discussed in the barn. You'll stay home until I come back."

The large man continued to stand gazing steadily at the floor as though he had heard nothing. Bertha spoke into the deep silence.

"He'll stay here, Sheriff."

Bill raised his eyes to her, perhaps more surprised than annoyed. Sheriff Hobart was not convinced, he needed more than her resolve so he waited for Bill to speak and did not remove his eyes from the larger and younger man.

Bill nodded, twisted to set the empty cup aside, turned back and nodded again. "I'll be here."

"You won't leave?"

"No. Not until you come back." Bill jutted his jaw in the direction of the closed bedroom door. "I can't leave him now, Blake."

The sheriff had not even been thinking of the

old man, but he was gratified now that *something* had come along to help him when he badly needed help.

He went to the door, turned and looked at Bertha. "You want me to ride back with you before I head for town?"

She was not going back just yet. "No thanks."

He shot Bill a final look and departed. Immediately afterwards the atmosphere in the parlor became increasingly troubled. She stoked the stove for warmth and watched with sidelong glances as he stepped to a window and stood massive and wide-legged, gazing stonily out into the settling night.

Then he left, crossing back to the barn where that little smoking lamp was still burning and while she went as far as the door to watch him disappear down there, she made no attempt to follow.

What tore at her heartstrings was the deluge of sorrow and sadness which God was unstintingly pouring down upon Big Bill. As though he were required to atone for something—something bad, extremely bad, and although she yearned to reach out to him, she was fearful. She did not know him well enough to know whether he needed comforting, nor was the fact that she was her father's daughter, and her brother's sister, influencing how he looked at her now.

Finally, she heated water and returned to bathe his father, to put him into a fresh nightdress, and to even comb his hair. All the while the old man watched her without making a motion to touch the slate, but when she was finished and was standing at bedside, he reached weakly, felt for her hand, and when she clung tightly, he tried his best to return the pressure, with a little but not very much, success.

She had never in her life wanted to cry as badly as she did at this moment, but she smiled through the scalding tears and remained with him until he seemed to want to doze, then she placed his hand gently atop the coverlets and retreated to the parlor—and by then she couldn't cry. Everything was there, the pain, the wrenching sorrow, the need for tears, but they simply would not come.

She went to the door, stepped out upon the covered porch to the very edge and watched the high, endless sky and after a while, replenished some way by this, she returned inside. The last thing she saw before closing the door was the faintest shimmer of lamplight down at the barn.

TWELVE
Dawn

She slept soundly in a slumped upright position in an old rocking-chair near the stove. Her first inkling of where she was, what had happened over here and why she was still there, arrived when she smelled fresh coffee and felt the cooling room begin to turn warm again. She opened her eyes.

Bill was at the stove expressionlessly stuffing kindling into the woodbox. She watched, yawned behind an upraised hand and said, "What time is it?"

He turned, pausing at work to study her for a moment. "Four in the morning. Why didn't you take one of the bunks. Jess didn't need his and I was busy all night. You'll have a crick in your back from sleeping sitting up like that."

She ignored the admonition to say, "Doing what—all night, Bill?"

She could have expected at least hesitation, had she been fully awake, but he answered straight back. "Burying them."

She stopped yawning and steadily studied him. "*Both* of them?"

"Yes. We got a little plot over on the slope where morning sunlight hits early each day. Maw's buried over there." He looked at her. "Tige's rider had some stuff in his pockets. I put it all in his hat." He pointed to an up-ended hat over near the door upon a little table. "His name was Clinton Anderson. I didn't make their boards because it was too dark. I'll make them today." He swung back to face her. "Care for some fried potatoes and meat for breakfast?"

She shook her head, marveling at him. "Are you going to eat?"

He shook his head. "No ma'm."

She arose, felt the thrust of back-pain exactly as he had predicted, and waited a moment before turning to cross to the bedroom door to look in.

Edson Black was lying as still as stone looking out the back-wall window with his good eye. He did not move until she stepped fully in and leaned closer, then he raised his glance, one side of his mouth tried valiantly to tug upwards a little, so she smoothed hair from his forehead, touched his hand, and half turned to go back out front to get him some broth—and it hit her as hard as a mule-kick. She slowly raised her eyes to that back-wall window. The old man lying there had an excellent view of the southerly turn of the yonder slope leading up from the meadow where the cabin was, and on around to where the gunfight had occurred yesterday. That view was also the same *for anyone returning.*

She gazed at Edson Black's profile for a moment, then gently closed the door and leaned upon it looking at Bill.

He sensed something and straightened up over at the stove where he had been setting the damper above the burning firebox. "There is. . . . ?"

"No," she said, "he's the same. Maybe even a little better." She strode as far as the center of the room. "Bill, when you brought Jess home yesterday across his horse, did you use that same

123

trail we both used riding over there from here, yesterday?"

He said, "Yes; there isn't any other decent trail to use. Why?"

"Because it can be seen for a long way from your father's window."

"Well, what of. . . . ?"

She saw understanding come slowly, and went to stand with her back to the firebox. She had become cold just recently. He did not look at her when he said, "You figure that's what caused him to break down last night?"

"Probably earlier than that, Bill, if he saw you bring your brother back. He could have been lying in there half out of his mind with sickness and grief—and we didn't know it."

They faced one another. He waited out a silent long moment before going towards the bedroom door, and although Edson was his father and she was an outsider, she said, "Wait; let me do it."

He offered no objection, but when she went into the room and picked up the slate, Bill filled the doorway behind her.

She asked her question in writing, waited a while to be certain his father understood, then erased the writing and inserted chalk into the old man's talon-like usable fingers.

They waited. The old man looked up at them, looked out the window where Stygian darkness was just now beginning to yield to new-day soft glow, and finally concentrated on the slate. He wrote, "Jess is dead. My wife's baby is dead. Father, I am ready . . . ready."

She turned, handed the slate to Bill, pushed out of the room and fled swiftly to the yonder porch out back; finally, she was able to cry.

An hour later she washed and combed her hair, kept her back to the big man donning his jacket by the door, along with his battered old stained hat, and when he left the house without speaking she made broth and took it into the bedroom for his father.

The old man sipped, which was more than she had expected, but nothing seemed able to shake him loose of his lethargy either during breakfast nor afterwards.

Later, she cleaned up; even cleaned the house with a broom, a whisk, and some rags she found in a cupboard. Even washed the windows until they sparkled with the new-day sunshine's brilliance.

Finally, exhausted, she walked out front and stood looking in the direction of Flesh-knife. Her brother knew where she was. Everyone, in fact, knew where everyone else was. This was a period of marking time. She pondered about Blake Hobart. She had never heard anyone say he was anything but a gun-handy plodding variety of lawman. She wondered where he was, now, and what he was doing. In her own judgment, what had happened, terrible as it was, had no malevolent basis.

She thought it was stupid, almost inexcusably bad reasoning which had brought the Flesh-knife cattle over here. And it was something akin in senselessness to have fierce Jess Black out there at the exact time those Flesh-knife riders appeared with the cattle.

It was, she told herself a set of incomprehensible circumstances when every element for something bad had been at hand waiting for a catalyst. If Jess had not been riding up there in among the trees, had not exploded with rage when he'd sighted the Flesh-knife cattle coming over onto Black rangeland, or if it had been Big Bill out there instead of Jess, there would have been no catalyst. The thing would have passed, even though it could have been a deliberate attempt to graze down Black grass, if there had been no Flesh-knife men out there when the cattle were discovered.

She turned at a heavy, muted sound and saw Bill standing there, coat draped from a mighty shoulder gazing at her. She smiled a little, tenderly. "Did you make the headboards?"

He nodded, stepped closer on the front porch and sank gently to the railing half facing away, half facing towards her. "Everything's different in daylight, isn't it?" he said, and flung the heavy coat over across a worn wooden bench.

"Things are easier to tolerate in daylight," she replied. There was nothing further for her to say to him. If they talked it would have to be at his initiative, so she waited, but Big Bill Black was never talkative, even under pleasant circumstances, so the silence ran on and on, until she decided to leave him alone out there on the porch, assuming this was his wish, but when she moved he stopped her by saying, "Bertha, I owe you."

She felt her face reddening. He had a very direct—and right now a very disconcerting—way of looking at people, sometimes, and under much more crucial circumstances she had met his stare without flinching, but this was so unexpected from him, it so thoroughly threw her off-balance that her gaze wavered.

He said, "I wanted to explain something . . . The reason I promised Blake to stay here, was not altogether because of Paw. I have no wish to kill your brother. Not even when it's an eye for an eye. Not for his sake, for *your* sake. I owe you his life."

She wondered at his ability to express himself. In an almost detached manner she studied him, seeing a man who was deeper and more talented than she had ever suspected. He was a large hulk of a man. That was how she had been thinking of him. This was his different side.

Then he went on speaking and scattered her thoughts. "You bathed him last night and combed his hair and you been doin' more'n my Maw could have done if she'd been alive."

His eyes never once left her face. She suddenly remembered how hard she had scrubbed and that her nose was probably as shiny as a sunbeam. This added to her self-consciousness. Normally, she was one of the least self-conscious people in the world.

"Bertha; I knew my brother. I know what Blake thought—maybe you thought it too—Jess forced that battle where they killed him. But I figured it through, and if they hadn't done that. . . ."

She was nodding her head so he let it trail off into soft silence between them. She said, "Isn't it usually like this? No one gets all the blame nor all the credit . . . The ranch cook knew Flesh-knife's rangeboss the year your father was killed, Bill. She told me several days back that our rangeboss was mean and scheming . . . What I'm saying is that he might have replaced my father's six-gun so that it looked as though your father murdered Weaver Johnson. I also knew my father, Bill." She paused a moment. "He was a man who—well—would force fights. That was a long time ago."

Bill nodded, clearly of the opinion that she was finished. She wasn't.

"Bill; I don't know what you think of laws of retribution or things like that . . . But why was it Jess up there yesterday instead of you, and why was it our present rangeboss who caused that, when all he knew of the past was bunkhouse gossip?"

Bill scowled slightly. He did not understand what she was driving at.

She did not elaborate. She turned to again consider the fresh new sun with its outpouring of molten gold.

He slouched upon the porch railing gazing at his scuffed boot-toes for a while. Finally he said, "You're tired. You've done more than enough. Bertha, I've got an old top-buggy in the barn I'll rig out and you won't have to worry your sore back riding a horse home."

She felt a little wrench of fondness, her first in a long while. He was a big, gentle, kindly and considerate man, but at first glance he was just big. She smiled down into his face.

"I'd have helped you with the headboards if you'd let me. And digging two graves all last night . . . Why don't you go inside and lie down? I'll be here if your father needs anything."

He glanced around the empty, hushed yard, over as far as the forested far slope where birdsong was coming faintly, and pushed upright off the groaning porch railing to stand close. "What do I do about all this?" he gently asked her.

She had the answer but she withheld it. *Nothing. Do nothing.* Leave it up to the law and Blake Hobart. She said, "Wait. You just wait, as

Blake wanted you to do. What good is another killing, whether it's deserved or not?"

He went to the door and scooped up his jacket, stood looking around at her for a moment, then wordlessly disappeared inside.

She had to exercise so she walked, first around the cabin then down to the barn, then out back to the corrals—and back there she caught the flash of brilliant morning sunlight off a pair of peeled-pole headboards far up in a yonder clearing to the east. It wrenched her heart but she stood a long while looking, before turning to see that he had cared for her horse and the beast was now corralled with feed and water, as happy and unconcerned as only non-human beasts can be.

She went back, avoiding the barn's interior, fearful he might have left the blood-flecked canvas lying there, reached the barn-front and stopped because distantly she thought she had caught sight of a horseman. It must have been an illusion because strain as she might she did not see it a second time.

Having exercised, she went across to the rear porch to fill the woodbox—which was filled from outside but which had a door opening inside the parlor in the interior wall. She finished that, drew water to scrub with again, patted her hair into place and leaned to open the door soundlessly.

Big Bill was sprawled dead asleep across one of the bunk-beds.

She eased out of her boots, left them on the porch and without a sound entered, eased the door closed, then went to the stove to heat food. Finally, she was able to eat.

Later, she took more broth to the old man. He was much better. That is, he turned his head when she entered without making a sound, and his good eye hinted at warmth at the sight of her, but otherwise his lethargic sorrow was still intact.

It had to have been almost a killing impact for him to be gazing out the window when one of his sons brought home the other of his sons dead and tied belly-down across a saddle.

She propped him, got broth down with more success that earlier, then wiped his face and sat down with the slate to print in large letters that he looked much better.

He took the chalk and scrawled, "What happened? How did it happen?"

She undoubtedly should have anticipated this, but the fact was that she hadn't. If she had, she would not have entered the room. But there was the question and the watering one good eye with its pain and its wonder.

She put the slate aside, took his usable hand to hold between both her palms, and began relating the facts as she knew them, without adding any of the bias nor conjecture which had by this time come to color every aspect of the gundown when his youngest son had died.

He clung to her hands, watched her face, did not offer to interrupt nor to reach for the slate when she had finished. He let his head roll to one side, away from her, as the silent grief brought a thin toll of tears down his blue-veined cheek.

She sat still keeping his chilled hand warm between her palms, and out in the parlor Big Bill shifted in his sleep, the bed groaned, but beyond that there was more of that enduring silence which had come the day before and would not depart for a number of other troubled days yet to come.

THIRTEEN
One Gunshot!

Three horsemen walking their animals southward crossed a mile out from the Black cabin in plain view and without paying much heed to the distant residence.

Bertha saw them first, as she was dishing up rabbit stew for Bill, and told him about them. Instead of stepping to a window Big Bill grabbed his carbine, crossed over and left the house by the rear door, and skirted along to the far edge of the porch to keep vigil.

Bertha was cold with fear. She was certain her brother would not do anything like this—or would he? She leaned at the window watching, and as those rangemen rode on southward

132

without turning aside, she settled back into a chair with relief.

When Bill returned she was dishing up his meal as though she had scarcely noticed the riders. He leaned his gun then said, "Grubliners, most likely, or hands lookin' for work."

She recalled that other rider, the one she had not been entirely certain she had seen earlier. When an opportunity arose she left the house under pretext and went for another short walk.

She tried hard to find any trace of that earlier horseman or any other rider, failed, and returned to the house satisfied.

But in the early afternoon a horseman was visible coming from the southeast, as though he may have penetrated those hills down there in order to reach the Black ranch.

He had done no such thing, and while something about the man was vaguely familiar to Bertha, watching from the rear porch, she kept her lips sealed.

Bill also watched, this time without the carbine. He had cleaned up and had shaved at the creek rather than at the house, had come directly from the creek, and had not gone inside where the Winchester was leaning.

Bertha finally said, "I think that's one of Tige's riders. But what would he be doing over here?"

Bill did not answer, he stepped back, eased the door aside, groped for the saddlegun, brought it forth and held it one-handed while he waited and watched.

But the Flesh-knife rider, if indeed Bertha were correct, may have spotted Bill with that gun because although he had ridden directly towards the cabin up to this point, now he veered westerly and passed along well in their sight without once raising his arm in the age-old horseman's salute.

They watched him head in the direction of the Flesh-knife's home-place, and Bertha shook her head in puzzlement. "What was the purpose of that?" she asked, and Bill was leaning aside the carbine when he answered.

"It might not have been a Flesh-knifer, just another saddle-tramp."

She would have taken an oath that had been a rider named Jett Smith. She leaned close to Bill looking along the side of the cabin, but now the rider was pushing his horse over into a lope; he was too distant to be recognized. When she pulled back Bill reached a big steadying hand, but she had been in no danger of tipping over the railing.

He freed her and turned towards the house, then turned back to say, "I don't want you to figure I'm not eternally grateful, or that I don't figure you'd ought to be over here all day. It's just that your brother can't approve of this, and there's nothing to do here but wait until Hobart gets back anyway."

"Your father," she reminded him, giving him look for look.

He let the topic drop right there, went inside, was in there only a short while and emerged with a double-barreled scattergun in the crook of an arm. "Birds," he said in response to her quizzical expression. "There's grouse up there near the graves as big and plump and sage-hens." He considered her a moment before saying, "If you weren't all bundled in skirts you could sure come along."

She did not want to 'come along,' she did not like to see birds and animals alive and sleek one moment, dead and broken the next moment, but after he was walking down alongside the barn on his way to the distant sidehill, she leaned there watching. His stride was long but graceful, the swing of his shoulders and torso was slight but noticeable. He was erect and powerfully formed. She went to the little back-wall bench to sit down, and consider some private thoughts.

She would never have confided them in anyone. Not even in her parents if they had been living, and in fact it was so unlike her to think of this, especially at this time, that she was disinclined to believe her own thoughts.

Finally, she saw a rider heading unerringly in the direction of the cabin, and this time he was coming from the northwest, from the direction of Frontera. She was willing to believe it was

Sheriff Hobart, and she was correct but he did not get close enough for full recognition for quite some little time.

She looked back towards the slope but Big Bill was nowhere in sight. She worried slightly about this, wondering how Blake Hobart would take it, that Big Bill was not at the house.

He took it very well, when she explained where Bill had gone, and tied up at the barn tie-rack listening to all the rest which she had to report. Then, when she stopped he leaned on the rack looking far out and around, but never in the direction Bill had taken.

He said, "By any chance either of you notice any riders around today?"

She explained about the three grubliners, or whatever they had been, then about the horseman she would have sworn was Jett Smith from Flesh-knife, but none of this apparently interested the lawman because as he was listening he was also turning, studying the sun-bright flow of endless grassland westerly, and the more occluded hill areas elsewhere. When she stopped speaking to watch him, he smiled and shook his head ruefully.

"Freeman was gone from Flesh-knife when I got back down there. Him and Ike." He seemed ready to defend himself to her. "They wasn't supposed to leave, and I had possemen over there, but they left. That's all there is to it."

She scowled. "Were you expecting to see them over here?"

"Miss, they was last seen heading east, which would be in this direction. Now, whether they veered off or not I can't rightly say, but the reason I cut things short at Flesh-knife and rode over here is because of something Claude said to another rider over yonder. He said someone owed for Clint Anderson."

She understood. "Big Bill?"

"I don't know. But Big Bill is left and his brother isn't. How would that look like to you?"

She had no view of it one way or another; she'd had no time to form much of an opinion, but she turned again to glance along the far hills where Bill had walked out of her sight, and because Sheriff Hobart was thinking positively about this situation, he hauled his horse around to get back astride for the short jog over where she had last seen Bill Black.

She watched him, too, then went to sit down trying to imagine Claude Freeman's frame of mind right now. He had never impressed her as a man who would feel obligated to avenge a commonplace rangerider to whom he was not even—to her knowledge anyway—a close friend.

She decided Blake Hobart was overly-sensitive; Claude and Ike would no doubt be well out of the countryside by now and still riding hard to widen the distance.

But regardless, one thing crossed her mind as she watched Sheriff Hobart working his way in and out of trees over yonder until he disappeared: Why had Claude run for it?

The implications were abundantly evident, and this bothered her anew because she had never before felt that the rangeboss had really intended to do more than perhaps steal a little grass.

She had never been allowed to know him very well, and this had been his choice not especially her choice. She was therefore unable to arrive at a fair conclusion.

She sighed, got to her feet to go inside and see if perhaps the old man was not ready for some nourishment, had her hand on the jamb, in fact, on one side, her other hand upon the smooth-worn edge of the slab door itself, when the flat, vicious snarl of a saddlegun broke the day-long hush.

Instinct caused her to recoil. Bill had taken a shotgun with him and although the sheriff had indeed had a booted carbine, the gunshot had not come from the direction she had seen the sheriff disappear, it had come from far to the left, over to the northeast of where Bill had gone, which was at least half a mile, and perhaps closer to a mile, from where Blake Hobart had passed from sight in among the lower tree-stands.

For a while there was no other sound. She closed the door and turned back facing the far-away hills, wondering, and beginning to fear very much that Blake Hobart's innuendo might have had a basis in fact; that gunman might have been Claude Freeman seeking his vengeance against Big Bill Black.

It did not make any sense to her, but then the longer she thought about it the more it was borne in upon her that no murder ever made very much sense, and the fact that Bill had not even been up there yesterday when the fight took place, fitted perfectly into this scheme she was now considering. There was no way under the sun for Claude nor his partner, Ike, the taciturn cowboy, to want revenge against Bill for what had happened—unless they wanted to stretch the bounds of reason right on out of all semblance to sense.

She entered the house remembering the old long-barreled rifle over a rack of antlers, heard noise in the old man's room, so for the moment forgot the old gun.

Edson was half out of the bed, scarlet in the face from straining, and when she caught him, set her legs and hoisted him back into his bed, she was surprised at how actually weightless he had seemed.

He made wet sounds with his mouth while frantically hunting the slate among the tumbled bedding. She handed it to him. He scrawled an almost undecipherable question.

"Who fired?"

She took the slate, pushed him back upon his pillows, argued with herself because she was not by nature a liar, but knew she was going to be one this moment, then wrote on the slate that Bill had gone hunting over across into the easterly hills, and raised perfectly calm eyes to meet his frantic stare.

It worked. She had not only been a successful prevaricator, she had also been a successful actress. He sank back, breathing in hard, shallow bursts.

Her conscience was outraged. She had deliberately misled an ill and dying man. Worse, if that gunshot had indeed been fired by the rangeboss of Flesh-knife, and the slug had hit Bill Black. . . .

She made the ailing man comfortable, smiled into his eyes, patted his hand and walked back to the parlor where her eyes fell upon the long-barreled rifle supported by a large rack of antlers near the front door.

She got the gun down, checked it for loads, found it had one slug in the chamber and was impressed by the size of the lead bullet. The bore of that old gun was large enough to accommodate the end of her finger easily. It probably had at one time been someone's buffalo rifle.

She went to the rear door, opened it and studied the far slope, saw nothing, no movement, no man-shapes, not even any worthwhile shadows, then movement at the barn turned her cold as she flung her stare in this fresh direction.

A saddled, bridled horse was standing there, head-hung in the lee-side shade, swishing his tail at flies as though he had been there hours.

It was the animal Sheriff Hobart had been riding. She unconsciously raised one hand to her throat, trying to see from where she was standing just inside the house, whether or not there was blood on Blake Hobart's saddle. She could not make any such determination from across the yard and instinct warned her not to step forth and walk down there.

The day was quiet, bright and pleasant, turning steadily warmer, and there was no hint of trouble at all—except for the utter hush throughout the entire area, even over as far as the sidehills, where there were no birds, not even any raucously scolding magpies nor jaybirds.

She considered. Women were usually safe in circumstances such as these. Usually. One wrong guess when people were armed and incensed could help fill a cemetery somewhere—or that little area over where the morning sun struck, where Big Bill had dug graves all last night.

On the other hand, she could not simply remain inside looking out. It was not her nature, nor would it have been desirable even if she had not been a decisive individual; the waiting was too drawn-out and corroding. She gripped the long rifle in both hands and stepped onto the porch, looked left and right and started down to the yard, then across it in plain sight under a dazzling sun.

The distance between house and barn was no more than three hundred feet. She felt it had to be at least half a mile. By the time she reached the front barn opening she was shaking.

There had not been a sighting nor a sound. If someone was out there . . . She went along the north barn wall to one of those windowless square openings where she could see Sheriff Hobart's horse without difficulty—and yes— there was blood on one skirt and a streak of it drying down one *rosadero*. But the horse was concerned only in dozing in barn-shade.

She left him out there, went down through to the rear of the barn, grounded her rifle and looked back towards the overgrown hillsides.

For a long while there was nothing to be seen, as before, but when she was blocking in specific areas and making a more detailed study she saw movement. It looked like a very large bear, the glimpse she caught, then it faced into shadows.

She knew how to aim and shoot a rifle, or a car-bine. That had been something she faintly recalled her parents arguing about. Her mother had been scandalized when her father took rifles, got her astride a horse when she had been no more than ten years old, had taken her out over the range many miles and had spent the entire day teaching her to hold a gun, to sight one, and finally how to shoot one.

She had practiced many times, so now as she sank slowly to one knee and sought a hand-rest upon the side of the barn's rear opening, she had the old rifle trained upon that moving shape up yonder, so that when it appeared again, ducking from hiding place to hiding place, she could follow it with little difficulty.

The bear emerged as a man, a very large man, larger in fact than Big Bill Black. It was not Claude Freeman nor Ike. She remembered them very well.

Then she caught her breath because it was not one man, it was Big Bill with the lawman slung over his shoulder!

She already knew Blake had been shot, so now the surprise was fleeting. She turned her attention next to what else might be back there, and saw nothing at all. But clearly Big Bill felt—or knew—there was an enemy back there because the closer he got to the open territory west from the slope down across grassland to the house and barn, the more he seemed clearly reluctant to step forth. She thought at first he was simply seeking some particular place to cross from. Then she could see what he was doing had to do with his desire to get down as far as possible while still being hidden by trees, before stepping forth to make his run for it.

Her heart sank. It was at least two hundred yards from the final tier of trees to the rear doorway of the barn. No one, even without carrying a burden, would be able to make that kind of a running crossing if there was anyone behind him waiting for him to show himself so they could shoot at him.

She straightened back to look southward where a small protruding spit of pines stood. She knew Bill was seeking that place even before she saw his big shadow filter down from above and get lost among the trees and ageless shadows of that place.

FOURTEEN
Fight!

He came to the very edge of the trees facing towards her. She saw him quite plainly and hoped whoever was behind him could not see him as well.

He shifted his hold on the limp lawman, strained left and right, then took one forward step as though testing something, the footing, his legs, or maybe even his wind.

He was not still carrying the shotgun, and in fact except for his holstered Colt she could see no indication of armament at all, so if he had found the sheriff's weapons in the woods he must have left them there.

He might just as well have; guns when a man was trying to run were a definite impediment.

She made up her mind where her obligation lay, nestled the rifle-stock closer to her shoulder and curled into it, regripped the door jamb with her free hand to provide a motionless rest, and gently lowered her head. The back sight was no-nonsense steel but someone had embedded ivory at the sighting tip of the front sight. It made aiming the long-rifle very easy.

Big Bill lunged ahead, got Hobart settled into his best-balanced position, and started forward picking up speed as he ran.

The distance was not great but it could have been half as long and not been any the less lethal for a man running with sweat coursing down his face, a dead weight across one shoulder.

Bertha clinched her eyes tightly closed, sprang them wide open, and concentrated upon the area of tree-shade and shadows Bill had departed from, rather than Bill himself.

For a long while she saw nothing. Then someone made a high, keening whistle and she snugged a finger around the trigger and waited.

The man came carelessly down through the trees to the forest edge and took aim while standing. Bertha squeezed off her shot. Lead struck tree-bark within inches of the man, tearing loose great, splintery bits of wood. The man's gunshot sailed high overhead as he was staggering backwards with one arm hurled up to protect his face and eyes from stinging wood-bark.

The rifle had made a noise like a cannon and its recoil was greater than any kick she had ever before received from a gun. She gasped from shock and pain, waited a moment before standing upright, then she leaned the old gun aside. It was no longer able to fire, there had been just that one huge cartridge in the chamber and she had not looked for more.

Bill was within a hundred yards of the barn opening. He saw her standing there, after that great, acrid scented cloud of black gunpowder smoke began to dissipate. She moved back to be less visible, and she did it just barely in time, because someone back up in the trees fired past Bill into the barn. She heard the singing bullet pass and strike solid wood with a meaty sound somewhere behind her.

She stepped completely clear of the doorway, hoping harder than she had ever hoped for any-thing he might make it, and he did, he came lum-bering into the barn breathing like a windbroke horse, stepped away from daylight and went down front to ease Blake Hobart to the ground. He had not even looked around at her on the way in, but after unburdening himself he pushed out a big hand to steady his body while he panted for breath, and slowly peered around.

She walked on up, knelt beside Hobart, leaned to gently turn his head so she could see the wound, and bit her tongue with anxiety. The bullet had not penetrated but it had ploughed alongside his head slicing through hair and flesh as though it had been a sharp knife. Hobart had bled like a stuck hog and was still bleeding when she looked up at Bill, her gently probing fingers finding no broken skull bone.

"Are there any clean rags out here?" she asked, and he straightened back nodding. He wordlessly walked away and she resumed her examination.

One thing seemed clear; whoever had fired at the lawman had tried for a head-shot, meaning they had tried to kill Blake Hobart.

Bill returned, passing down to her several rags. He had also brought back a tin of saddle-gall salve. She put that aside and went to work creating a compress-bandage which would hopefully assist in stopping the flow of blood, although by this time the bleeding had stopped of its own accord in most of the lengthy wound. It dripped and it was turning mottled purple and it was swelling tremendously. It was going to leave a distinct scar even though Hobart—if he survived—might re-arrange his hair to cover it.

When she had made the unconscious lawman as comfortable as possible, had completed the bandaging and had dipped water from a stone trough out front to wash his face and try to get most of the blood off, she cleansed her own arms and hands then went back where Bill was standing in a shadowy place studying the distance.

She said, "Did you see him?"

"Not *him,*" he informed her, "*they.* There are two of them. The one that got Blake was over to the north. I didn't know anyone was closer than the house when he cut loose. Maybe he was stalking me, in which case Blake saved my life by getting himself shot."

She peered out. "Where is the other one?"

He pointed. "Was northeast up the slope not too far from the buryin' ground, but after the shot, and after Blake fell, that one came down towards me making more noise than a bull in a hayfield. I got into hiding, and after a while snuck around to where Blake was and hoisted him." He looked down into her white face, and chuckled as he raised a hand to gently squeeze her right shoulder. She flinched.

He said, "Yeah, I know how that is. I learned to aim using that old buffler gun, and ever' time I'd get ready to pull the trigger I'd start to cry because I knew it was going to topple me over backwards, and it always did." He looked at the old rifle. "Until today, I hated that darned old thing."

She tried to smile but she could not be as nonchalant as he was being, and when he saw her glance drift worriedly back towards the far sidehill he sighed and also turned back, no longer smiling.

A moment later he said, "We'd better get Blake into the house before they figure some way to get down to the south of us here, in the trees, and cover the yard too."

He had Hobart's blood all over his upper clothing. She was awed by the amount of blood Sheriff Hobart had shed.

She went out front to look first, and when he walked up carrying the sheriff in his arms as though Hobart were a small child, she looked at him and said, "How many times do you get to do this without being hit?"

He considered the back of the house a few hundred feet distant, took a fresh grip on his burden and when she nodded he struck out. It was an uneventful crossing. She ran over behind him and they both entered the house in a rush, a trifle breathless, not from the meager distance but from the tightness in each chest over the situation they were in.

Bill put Hobart upon one of the bunk-beds and turned back for his carbine just inside the door. Bertha went to work taking the blood-soaked shirt and jacket, neckerchief and undershirt, off the sheriff. Hobart groaned. She brought warm water from the stove and scrubbed his naked upper body clean. He opened his eyes, which did not focus, and until she had finished, had put him into one of Big Bill's shirts, which fit like a horseblanket, he seemed aware of what was being done to him but he was obviously incapable of focusing upon the person who was doing it.

She went to the old man's room, lingered very briefly and returned to close the door, leant upon it for a moment with both eyes closed, then shake herself and go after a cup of coffee which she took to Bill over near the rear door.

She smiled at him. He smiled back and accepted the coffee. She had something to tell him, but as with all things there was, and was not, a time, so she simply stood close to him tired out on her feet, and when he leaned to softly say there was some corn whisky in a jug at the base of the cupboard near the stove, she understood.

"As soon as he can swallow I'll get some down him . . . Sheriff Hobart, I mean."

He was turning away when she said that, and slowly turned back, slowly brought intelligent gun-metal eyes to bear fully upon her face.

"Bertha . . . Paw?"

She smiled softly, lay a hand upon his sleeve, and without saying a word turned towards the cupboard. He leaned the carbine and followed her progress with his eyes, then lifted the carbine and resumed his vigil when someone off in the middle distance, perhaps out behind the barn, rattled some stacked wood.

He had just one place at the house where he

could see down through the barn from front to back. Otherwise, the barn being slightly out of alignment with the house, its interior was not subject to a good view.

He walked to the distant corner of the parlor, leaned to lift the loophole cover and put his eye to it. She was not watching so she did not see him step back toss his hat aside and very gently raise the carbine to insert the barrel with plenty of room all around it, until it was protruding from the rear of the house.

Then he waited. It was a long wait, too, but not because he had seen no one, rather because he *had* seen them but they never stood for more than a moment in one place.

One did, finally.

Bill aimed, held his breath, and fired. Bertha almost jumped out of her boots and the sound even brought a sudden violent response from Sheriff Hobart, so she had to go over and hold him to the cot with both hands until the fright passed.

He stared at her from one puffy, bluish eye, and one perfectly normal eye. This time his sight was dead-steady. He knew who she was.

He said, "Help me up!"

She continued to lean her solid weight upon him using both hands. "You lie right where you are."

He groaned. The pain was more than simply

physical, torn-flesh-pain, it was also something inside his head which hurt with all the complete anguish of the biggest hangover anyone had ever had or could ever have imagined. He was no match for Bertha Johnson right at this moment so she held him down without much trouble, until Bill fired again, then he was as aggravated and startled as before.

She watched Bill withdraw the Winchester and lean it as he gazed around the room. She finally eased off and went to get the whiskied coffee. She got it and took it back, saw Bill moving diagonally towards the closed door and while she helped Sheriff Hobart drink, she watched as Bill entered the room, lingered, then returned and without glancing towards her returned stony-faced to the place where he had left the carbine.

Blake Hobart's recovery was unquestionably hastened by that heavy jolt of corn whisky in his black java. He sat up—and immediately dropped his head into both hands as the triphammers started pounding worse than before inside his head.

Bertha got more laced coffee and took a cup to Bill. He nodded his appreciation, tasted it, looked at her, then tasted it again. She could shoot a rifle, winnow illness from the sick, nurse the injured, and even clean up a boar's-nest of an old lived-in log house, and still look handsome throughout every bit of it, but she had never been taught not to overload coffee cups when she laced them.

He said, "I was just thinking. I'm the only Black left. First my brother, and now Paw." He drained the cup and handed it back. "Why am I doing this, Bertha? I shot a man a few minutes ago inside the barn. Why am I fighting them—I don't feel I'd ought to be doing that."

"It's your land, Bill. It was your brother they killed."

He nodded and would have turned back but she detained him with a strong grip. When their eyes met this time she raised up as high as she could and planted a warm kiss squarely on his cheek, then as she dropped back down she said, "I hate it too; I hate everything about anything as ridiculous and vicious and senseless as this is. But they won't stop will they? Then we can't stop either."

He lifted his free hand to trace out a shadow along the side of her face. It was a gentle, bittersweet little caress and she would have stood there throughout Eternity, but someone savagely pumped three bullets into the front of the wood near where they were standing, and he turned her away with the same hand, but this time it was not quite as gentle.

He waited, then leaned to peek out. There was no one in sight, naturally, but there was gunsmoke dissipating near the barn's front entrance so he continued to lean and wait.

Whoever that was had no intention of giving up, otherwise, if he'd felt badly over having his partner shot down moments earlier, he no doubt would have gone out back, climbed over leather and lit out southward keeping the barn between himself and log house.

Instead, he shot again, this time from outside the barn to the northward, and this time the bullet struck within inches of Bill's loophole, forcing Bill to spring back and flinch.

FIFTEEN
Riders!

Sheriff Hobart was a hindrance and Bertha told him so. "You can't do anything. You can't even see straight nor stand up, so lie here and be quiet!"

He peered from one watery eye down the room where Bill was standing. He clearly had something to say but Bill fired again and the noise inside the house was so deafening Hobart flinched and took Bertha's advice, he sank back and remained motionless for a while.

Bertha was at the front of the room when she caught movement far out and stiffened quickly into an upright position. It was two riders fogging it in a belly-down run brandishing six-guns as they recklessly charged forward. One of them she knew even at that distance—Tige. She assumed

154

the other one had to be Jett Smith, the rider who had been over here earlier.

Farther back, so distant she could not at first make them out at all, just their clouds of rising dust, were three more horsemen, but they would not be able to get anywhere near the Black place for another hour, while those two charging gun-wielders were going to arrive within minutes.

She crossed to Bill and sent him to the front of the house to see for himself. She went with him and when he swore under his breath she put a strong hand upon the arm holding his Winchester. "Give my brother a chance to prove what he's doing over here."

Bill straightened back and considered her face before saying, "All right. For you I'll do that and heaps more." He forced a reassuring smile. "They can't do much more than spend bullets against the log walls, can they?"

He leaned down to look out again. Now, Tige and his rider were veering towards the south side-wall of the house as though they meant to charge on around into the area of the barn.

Bill crossed the room, back to his loophole to watch, and what happened stunned him.

Her brother was a couple of yards in the lead as he and his companion swept around into the area between the rear of the house and the front of the barn. Tige did not seem to hesitate, he drove his horse straight at the front barn opening. Someone over there turned to run, to stumble clear, and Bill saw them fleetingly, knew it was the surviving bushwhacker, then three guns exploded almost simultaneously, moments later another gun exploded twice, very deliberately and at very deliberate intervals.

Bill strained to see past the smoke. One riderless horse came back out of the barn, spooked, and head high. Bill stepped over and yanked back the door to go out for a better view, he raised the cocked Winchester though and held it like that, waiting for whatever would happen next.

Tige came to the doorway limping, ivory-handled Colt in his hanging fist. He saw Bill and nodded towards him. The other Flesh-knife rider walked his excited horse past Tige, out into the sun-bright yard. It was indeed the stocky rider named Jett Smith, and evidently he was also nerveless because as he turned towards the tie-rack to swing off, he casually holstered his Colt, lifted his hat and mopped forehead-sweat with a soiled cuff, then turned his back on Big Bill to dismount and loop his reins.

The sound of Bertha coming into the doorway at his back made Bill turn slightly. When she saw her brother she called to him. "You are supposed to be at home! Those were the sheriff's orders!"

He said, "Yeah. But Jett saw some skulkers in the foothills and we figured they would kill *him,* and maybe *you,* so we just had to outrun his possemen." Tige limped forward still holding his cocked Colt downward, still watching Bill's hand near the carbine's trigger guard. "You all right, Bertha?"

She smiled out at him. "I'm all right, Tige. The sheriff is in here wounded." She regarded the big man nearby. He slowly lowered his Winchester and eased off the dog as he said, "Who's in the barn?"

Tige limped to the very edge of the porch before replying. "Claude Freeman, my range-boss." He met Bill's gaze. ". . . Dead."

After an interval of silence Tige also said, "I don't know why he did it. I really don't."

Bertha pushed past and leaned to take the ivory-stocked Colt from her brother's hand and drop it into his hip-holster. He looked at her. "He hated these people over here, but hell he wasn't even in the country when Paw got killed . . . It had to be just the talk that made him hate them this much. He told me—I made him tell me last night—why he brought the cull-cut up here. He figured there might be firing and he figured using the cull critters as a shield even if some were killed Flesh-knife would still be able to get this land real cheap . . . They killed one Black on purpose and he said with any kind of luck he'd get the other one, then I'd have all the land I'd need and maybe even think about some sort of partnership with him . . . Sis, he was crazy. Crazy as a damned pet 'coon."

157

She raised her eyes when Big Bill left the carbine and stepped off the porch on his way to the barn. She would have trailed after but her brother gripped her arm and shook his head.

"Claude's in there and he ain't nice to look at, Sis."

But Jett Smith accompanied Big Bill Black into the barn. Where Bill halted to see the pair of dead men, the one named Ike which he had shot from the loophole, and the former rangeboss beside him, Jett sprayed amber, shifted his cud of tobacco and said, "Mister, you're plumb lucky it seems to me you got friends like the Johnsons."

Bill looked around. Jett chewed and returned the look without batting an eye. He was not very tall and he was approaching the age when he could no longer ride out as well nor as long and hard as he once had been able to, but he was absolutely fearless.

Bill did not say a word, he turned and went back across the yard. Tige knew of the other death by this time; Bertha had told him. Tige arose and stood on his good leg, the other one had been twisted slightly when he'd sailed off his horse inside the barn. He offered Bill a soiled hand. "I'm sorry about your Paw," he said.

Bill took the hand, pumped it and released it as he solemnly said, "I understand. I'm sorry about *your* Paw and I have been for a lot of years . . . And maybe now that they're both gone . . . ?"

Tige smiled. "Sure. As for the damage—I'll make it good. Sure, I talked about your land, but only to buy it or maybe lease it. I never even hinted to Claude we'd get it this way. Never even hinted. I couldn't believe it when they told me he'd driven our cull-cut up here onto you."

Bill nodded belief and Bertha came over to stand beside him. She felt for his hand, slipped her fingers inside his palm, and he gently closed his hand around in a gentle squeeze. She squeezed back and leaned a little so they were touching elsewhere.

Those possemen came streaming into the yard glaring at Tige and Jett Smith. From the doorway where he had just appeared to lean, sickly Sheriff Hobart looked at his possemen and said, "Hell of a fine bunch you are. Couldn't even keep two cowmen over where they belonged!"

One of the possemen, a small-time cowman from over nearer Frontera, was eating an apple from a shirt-pocket when he said, "Blake; two-bits a day riding for the law don't include maybe getting *shot* too, does it?" He winked at Bertha and she smiled back.

She and Big Bill were still touching, were still holding hands where the others could not see it, so when Tige said, "Sis; they got any coffee around this place?" she was very reluctant to move. But she did it, she freed her fingers and headed for the log house—one more time.

Center Point Publishing
600 Brooks Road ● PO Box 1
Thorndike ME 04986-0001 USA

(207) 568-3717

US & Canada:
1 800 929-9108
www.centerpointlargeprint.com